Nothing made any sense anymore, Finn thought

Finn had ridden twenty-story roller coasters that threw him around less than the emotional ride he was currently experiencing with one Diana Song.

At the moment, with her full, pillow-soft lips pressing against his, her leanly curved body molding to him with only a thin silk robe as a barrier...well, he wasn't complaining.

He had been furious at her, ready to yell at her until she saw reason, when he got to her door. The thought of her betrayal and her cold-blooded handling of his friend Lincoln was still enough to keep him at least a little sane. But there was something about her that had him addicted to her like something chemical, illegal, totally uncontrollable.

Add to that the fact that she was now kissing him as if her life depended on it and it pretty much wiped away everything else he'd been feeling, except for the confusion and pure, primal heat.

Diana was probably still gunning for him, for Lincoln and the Club, so why, when she'd reached for him, had his body so enthusiastically answered the call?

How could he be so hot for a woman who was his worst enemy?

Dear Reader,

I have to say...Finn is my favorite.

There is just something so *fun* about a "wardrobe-challenged" billionaire with a wicked sense of humor who wants to live as if he's dying. Life's a game, and he's the ultimate Player.

Of course, now he's up against Diana "The Hammer" Song, his father's determined legal counsel. She doesn't believe in games, but she does play to win.

This book concludes the Player's Club trilogy, finally revealing the origins of the secret society and bringing us full circle. This series has been a complete blast to write, and I hope it's been just as fun to read!

Enjoy!

Cathy Yardley

Cathy Yardley

THE PLAYER'S CLUB: FINN

TORONTO NEW YORK LONDON
AMSTERDAM PARIS SYDNEY HAMBURG
STOCKHOLM ATHENS TOKYO MILAN MADRID
PRAGUE WARSAW BUDAPEST AUCKLAND

ISBN-13: 978-0-373-79678-6

THE PLAYER'S CLUB: FINN

This edition published by arrangement with Harlequin Books S.A.

For questions and comments about the quality of this book please contact us at Customer_eCare@Harlequin.ca.

www.Harlequin.com

Printed in U.S.A.

ABOUT THE AUTHOR

People think Cathy Yardley was crazy to trade sunny Southern California for the rainy Pacific Northwest. Fortunately, she firmly believes that writing isn't a job for sane people. Now happily writing in the wilds of Seattle, she loves hearing from readers. To do so, email her at cathy@cathyyardley.com.

Books by Cathy Yardley

HARLEQUIN BLAZE

14—THE DRIVEN SNOWE
59—GUILTY PLEASURES
89—WORKING IT
300—JACK & JILTED
332—ONE NIGHT STANDARDS
366—BABY, IT'S COLD OUTSIDE
662—THE PLAYER'S CLUB: SCOTT*
668—THE PLAYER'S CLUB: LINCOLN*

*The Player's Club

To Kathryn Lye, Annelise Robey
and Christina Hogerbe, for acting as midwives
to this trilogy. You guys made this possible.
Thanks for being there for me.

1

FINN MACALISTER LEANED BACK and took in paradise.

The sky was an impossible blue, the water a silky turquoise rushing back to a stretch of white sand, dotted with jade-green palm trees. He'd been to Oahu several times, but it was as if he'd never seen it before in his life.

"Paddle!" Benji, the twenty-two-year-old next to him, yelled like a drill sergeant. *"Paddle your ass off, damn it!"*

Without thinking, Finn cut into the water with his hands and…well, paddled his ass off.

The wave was bearing down on him like a freight train. Making it worse, it was a ten-foot-tall freight train, roaring at him, eager to pummel him against the hidden coral reefs somewhere down in that beautiful water he'd been waxing rhapsodic about. He paddled and cursed and finally managed to get his ass, and his board, over the ridge as Benji signaled his intent…and headed right for the danger zone.

Benji was paddling like a champion swimmer, attacking the wave like an ant attacking a tank. He got on, starting the ride, hitting it like a champ. Finn found himself holding his breath as he watched Benji go… watched him hit the sweet spot like something out of *The Endless Summer* as he shot the curl, the translucent sheet of water closing behind him as he shot forward like a bullet out of a Colt 45. And he caught a glimpse of the broad, absolutely foolish smile that plastered the kid's face. He let out a primal scream of joy.

Finn let out a breath. *There you go, kid.*

"Welcome to the Player's Club," Finn said to no one in particular. Then he glanced back at the next wave. It was rising like a monster.

His heart kicked up a little, and a small smile sneaked onto his face.

He'd surfed plenty of times. He wasn't a pro or anything, but he wasn't a rank amateur. And sure, Finn had told Lincoln he was only going to be there to make sure nothing happened to their latest pledge, Benji. Of course, Benji was a semipro surfer, base jumper and all-around badass. Pretty good for a kid.

But Finn wasn't doing what he was doing because he was jealous, or even because he wanted to show he could still do everything he could do before he'd turned thirty.

He felt his nerves tingle, his body almost shiver with the excitement of anticipation. The delicious, almost narcotic feeling of thrill danced along his skin.

This, he thought. *This is what I need.*

And he signaled, moving on the wave.

He thought he heard some yelling in the distance.

The lifeguards he'd hired specifically were probably plenty pissed at him. Benji seemed to be cheering him, though, and that was encouraging, especially as he almost bobbled getting onto the surfboard.

It was…well, he hadn't ever ridden a dragon, but if he ever found himself accidentally leashing and then riding a dragon in some weird dragon-rodeo, it would feel exactly like this. The water was screaming past him, and he saw the crest of it, curving over him, like the center of a cyclone, trying to swallow him up.

His entire life focused like a laser point. In that moment, he wasn't the only son and heir to the multi-billion-dollar Macalister candy fortune. He wasn't the cofounder of the supersecret Players' Club. He wasn't the scared and spindly six-year-old with the illness that made his family treat him so strangely.

He was just Finn.

He broke through, shooting out, watching the beauty of the curl, feeling triumphant. He shouted, pumping his fist in the air.

Then, there was a loud, cracking sound and a violent jolt as his board snapped. The wave let loose its own triumphant roar, grabbing a hold of him, tight as a fist. Suddenly, the beautiful blue water was surrounding him, choking off all his air and spinning him like a washing machine. He felt a panic, felt the hard slice of something against his head.

He had two thoughts in the space of a millisecond.

One, that as Lincoln had warned this had been one of his stupider ideas…one that might very well kill him.

And two, that even now, he probably would have made the very same choice.

Better to die feeling alive than live feeling dead.

And with that cheerful thought, everything went black.

"DID YOU ENJOY DINNER tonight, Diana?"

"It was lovely," Diana Song said, smiling with encouragement as she accepted the paper-thin glass of Pinot Noir. Truthfully, she barely remembered the place: some Thai restaurant, artsy and secluded. Her mind hadn't been on the food.

"I'm glad we decided to come back to your place," her date, Travis, said as he sat down next to her on her couch. He stroked her shoulder, his eyes alight with anticipation.

She looked away for a second, taking a quick sip of the wine. It was expensive, sophisticated—much like Travis.

I really should have brought the Peterson file home.

She closed her eyes for a second. No. She wasn't going to think about work tonight. She wasn't going to screw this up by getting distracted.

She was going to have *sex* tonight, damn it.

She'd been on six dates with Travis. Granted, they'd been spread out over four months, but still...that was practically a relationship.

For her, considering her track record, that was practically *marriage.*

She forced herself to gaze into his eyes. "I'm glad we came back here, too."

"You know," he said, leaning close enough that she could smell his cologne, "I admire you for your reputation at Macalister, but getting to know you… You're so much softer, more approachable than I would've thought." He nuzzled her jawline. "So much sexier."

He'd pitched the words in a sensual tone, was obviously moving in, but something he said caught her attention. "What reputation?"

He laughed at that, pulling back. "They call you Macalister's Hammer. I don't think you got that nickname because you enjoy carpentry as a hobby."

She stiffened, putting her drink down on her glass coffee table. She loathed that nickname. "I'm just a lawyer. Just because I'm good at my job some people might think that means I'm…tough, whatever."

He looked immediately contrite. "I'm sorry. I didn't mean—I'm not trying to say you're tough, or cold, or any of the other crap they say at the office."

She stared at him.

This is so not helping me decide to invite you into bed, pal.

Sure, she'd brought him home with the idea of them moving on to the next step. Frankly, right now, he was the only candidate she had. He was attractive, easy enough to talk to without being too insistent. He worked in the patent office at Macalister Enterprises, pushing through patents for candy. Yes, candy. She'd met him at some company meeting, liked the look of him and the fact that he seemed interested.

Now she was wondering if maybe she hadn't set the

bar a bit low. Convenience and some superficial traits might not be the best barometer of bedmates.

He was nipping at her earlobe, and her mind kept whirring away. Yes, she was currently in a year-and-a-half sexual drought, but once she'd made it a year, it didn't seem as urgent anymore. She leaned against the back of her couch, wondering how she'd never noticed before how uncomfortable it was. Of course, she was rarely home, and didn't spend a lot of time loafing on the couch.

Maybe it was just that *she* was uncomfortable.

"So..." He stroked his fingertips along her arm, tracing up to her shoulder. "Where were we?"

He leaned forward, his lips brushing over hers. She tried. So help her, she tried. It wasn't bad, but it completely lacked the sexual zip that she was hoping for. He seemed to sense it, too, but instead of acknowledging it, he redoubled his efforts, giving it the full court press.

She winced uncomfortably when he started plunging his tongue into her mouth. When she backed off, their breathing was ragged, his with arousal, hers in a desperate attempt to get more air.

Come on, Diana, she chided herself. *You may not get a second chance at this. Did you really want to spend another night by yourself with a pint of Häagen-Dazs and a crappy chick flick?*

"Come on, Diana," he echoed, as if reading her mind. "We both know where this is going. We've been headed here for months. Why don't we go into the bedroom, see where it takes us?"

Unless you're hung like a Louisville Slugger and you've got some caramel-gingersnap ice cream on you, I seriously doubt it.

He tugged her hand, leading it down to the bulge growing in his pressed pin-striped trousers. Well, it wasn't a slugger, but it wasn't a pencil, either, she thought, slowly stumbling back into the mood. Besides, she could always provide her own ice cream.

She kissed him again, dodging when he tried to get too intense, but still trying to get in the mood. Her breasts tightened beneath the new black-lace bra she'd bought the weekend prior, with just this date in mind.

This could happen, she thought. *This could really...*

"What the hell is that?" he asked, glancing around the room.

"What are you talking about?"

"That sound. It's like an alarm or something. What is that?"

She wanted to scream. Obviously, she wasn't that good a kisser if he could be distracted by—

Then she heard what he was talking about. It was a song, tinny and blaring and growing increasingly louder: the Rolling Stones' "Can't Get No Satisfaction."

She bounced off the couch. "My cell phone."

"Didn't you turn it off?" He sounded offended at her oversight. "Never mind. Let it go to voice mail."

"Can't. This is probably important." She grabbed the still-ringing cell phone. That particular ringtone was her boss's private line. If she let the call go to voice mail, he would be pissed. "Hello? Hello?"

"Diana." Her boss, Thornton "Thorn" Macalister, sounded pissed anyway. "There's been an emergency."

All her ardor cooled. "What happened?"

"Finn."

She closed her eyes, gripping the cell phone tight. It was ten o'clock at night and an emergency. One that required Thorn calling her from his private line. So *of course* it was Finn Macalister, the black sheep, the recalcitrant son.

"Need me to post bail again?" she asked, rubbing at her temple and noticing the tension between her shoulder blades. "Or…"

"He's in the hospital."

She stiffened. "I'm sorry. How bad? What can I do?"

"Don't know. We're flying out tonight to see for ourselves." Thorn's voice was filled with fury and sadness, mixed with frustration. "He could've gotten killed. Betty's having a nervous breakdown, and I don't know how many more of these episodes we can take."

Finn was known for his stunts, although his parents usually found out about them after the fact when he was safe and sound. The guy had the devil's own luck. Diana was surprised he'd survived this long, given what she'd heard about his exploits. She'd only seen him at a few family functions, since he rarely showed up at the Macalister corporate headquarters—even though he was on the board of directors.

She thought of his face. That handsome, boyish face, that quick, wicked, sexy smile. She remembered him at the Macalister mansion once. In swim trunks. With a rock-hard bod.

She sighed. Such a shame, on so many levels.

"What do you need me to do, Thorn?"

"Several things, I suppose." Her normally blustering, pushy boss sounded defeated. "I need you in Oahu, as soon as possible. Betty and I are already in the air. I'm sending a driver to your place. Car should arrive in twenty minutes—you can take the other company plane. Betty didn't want to wait for you. We'll discuss plans when you get there."

"Fine. I'll be ready." She wasn't surprised when he hung up abruptly. She closed the phone, her head already clicking into business mode. She glanced over at Travis. "I'm sorry. We'll have to reschedule."

"What?" He looked aghast. "Just like that?"

Because she'd already switched over, she largely ignored Travis as she started gathering what she would need with her. "It's a crisis. Macalister crisis. I'm not sure how long it's going to take to clear up, and I've got a car coming in twenty minutes. I'm afraid we'll have to maybe do this another time?"

She probably could have asked that with more enthusiasm.

"That was Thornton Macalister? The big guy himself." Travis stood up. His pants were definitely sporting an obvious bulge that was deflating fast. "I don't work with him directly, but my boss says he's, uh, challenging. Does he do stuff like this often?"

"Stuff like what?" She headed to her hall closet, calling over her shoulder. She had two roller bags: one filled with warm weather clothes, one with cool. She grabbed the warm weather overnighter, jogged into her bedroom and added a suit bag. Last but not least was her laptop case that she pulled from the desk.

Just like that, she was packed. She'd done this drill before.

Travis stared at her quickly assembled gear. "He tells you you're going to be on a plane in twenty minutes," he said, surprised, "and you're ready in less than two? He calls at ten o'clock at night and you tell your date to just go home?"

"That's why they pay me the big bucks."

Travis was frowning, and she realized he wasn't quite ready to leave yet. Maybe she'd have him walk her out when the town car got there to take her to the airstrip. "Ever thought about telling him no? That you've got a life?"

"Why would I do that?" It was as if he were suddenly speaking Swedish. "Is this just because I can't sleep with you now?"

Wrong button to push. He looked offended, his back straightening. "Hard as it is to believe, I'm actually able to have sex with other people. And do. Frequently."

She blinked. "Okay, yuck."

He scowled. "That wasn't...damn it. My point was, I made a point to pursue you, despite other possibilities. I thought you might be interesting to start a relationship with. You're intelligent, powerful, ambitious—obviously, to be able to get to where you are at such a young age."

"Well, ambition and power don't exactly happen if you keep saying no to the boss, Travis." Now she was really glad she hadn't slept with him.

"I guess on some level, I'm not going to want to keep coming in second to another man."

She piled her bags by the door. "It's not like that with Thorn."

"No, you're right. It's the job." He laughed ruefully. "But...well, now that I'm seeing it, I don't know that I'd want to keep coming in second to that, either."

"That's really sexist, you know," she said, with more weariness than anger. She glanced at her cell phone's time display—fifteen minutes. "I'm not the only one here who's been too busy. Were you planning on scaling back your hours to give our 'relationship' the time it deserved?"

"Touché," he said. "Well, then. I guess we don't have anything else to say."

"Guess not." She opened the door. "Have a nice night."

He stared at her for a long moment. At some point, she knew he was waiting for an apology.

She stared back. As he'd noted, they didn't call her the Hammer for a carpentry fetish.

He broke first, and she lost a notch of respect for him. Then he stalked out, and she shut the door behind him.

She sighed again. So much for sex. At least she had work, right?

Yeah, she thought sarcastically. Work was *waaaay* better than sex.

2

FINN WOKE UP IN THE HOSPITAL with a mild sense of anxiousness.

Oh, crap, not again. He reached up, felt his aching head. There was a new, jagged scar up in his hairline... but he had hair. He had eyebrows, he thought, tracing his face. Then, abruptly, it all came back to him.

Hawaii. Surfing. The Pipeline.

"Good morning," his best friend, Lincoln, said, sitting on a plastic chair next to the hospital bed. "And how are we feeling?"

"Peachy, although would you check my wallet? 'Cause I swear, I think I was mugged," Finn said, laughing. He noticed immediately that Lincoln didn't join in. "Okay, not one of my better jokes..."

"Not one of your smarter moves," Lincoln interrupted.

Finn frowned. "This isn't going to be one of your Big Papa Lincoln lectures, is it? Because my head hurts enough as it is."

Lincoln shook his head. "I'm concerned, Finn. For you, and for your pledge, Ben."

Now that had Finn sitting up, even though his body yelped in response. "I would never do anything to endanger anyone, and you damned well know it."

"Not stopping someone is a kind of endangerment," Lincoln returned.

"Ben's a strong surfer and a solid swimmer. Besides, I had EMTs on the beach just in case."

"How very forward thinking of you," Lincoln said. "Were they really for him, though? Because you know you could've just stayed with them on the beach and fulfilled your duties as a mentor."

Finn scowled. "Where's the fun in *that*?"

"I do understand. But..." Lincoln paused. "You scared us, man. And this kid, Ben—where the hell did you find him?"

Finn shrugged. "BASE jumping off Hoover dam. For being only twenty-two, the kid's got skills and he's only going to keep—"

"So why does he need us?"

The question stopped him. "I don't know. He thought we sounded cool. He'd heard of us. He'd made the connection."

"A lot of people are beginning to make the connection between you and the Club," Lincoln pointed out, then held up his hands at Finn's murderous glare. "Just saying."

"I haven't told anybody who I didn't make a pledge," Finn said, then ignored Lincoln's head-shaking. "I haven't invited *that* many pledges. And I haven't broken any rules. You know I'm not in this for the glory, Lincoln."

"I know," Lincoln said. "But Ben's challenges sound reckless."

"Oh, come on, Linc. We haven't lost anybody yet."

"There's always a first time." Lincoln sighed. "And I hate the idea that it's going to be you."

Finn gritted his teeth. He wasn't quite sure what to say. Fortunately, he didn't have to. Juliana, Lincoln's stunning girlfriend and one of his fellow Players, popped into the room.

"Parents headed this way." She walked over and kissed Finn on the cheek. Then punched him on the shoulder. "You're an asshole."

"Ow! What the hell?"

"Bad enough you're a thrill-seeker, but that kid you tagged has a death wish," she said darkly. "Come on, Linc. I do *not* want to have a conversation with the Macalisters."

Lincoln nodded, standing beside her and studying Finn. "We'll talk about this when you get back to San Francisco. I'll have somebody pick you up, bring you over to Tucker's condo on Turtle Bay."

"All right." Finn watched as they slipped out like shadows. He didn't really have time to brace himself before his parents showed up.

His father was wearing a blue polo shirt and a pair of slacks, looking oddly rumpled—they probably came over straight from their flight, Finn thought with a twinge of guilt. His mother's face was totally pale. He wondered if they'd gotten any sleep.

"How did you hear?" he asked, instead of saying hello.

His father's expression was dark and ominous. "Did you really think you could keep it from me?"

"I thought we'd agreed—no more private investigators tailing me, after I lost the last five." Why had he even trusted that agreement with his father, let his guard down? If he'd lost the tail they'd put on him this time, he could've avoided this whole scene.

"I thought you'd finally stopped pulling stupid stunts like this," his father shot back. "Guess we were both wrong."

Finn didn't want this to devolve into one of their usual arguments. Sitting naked in a thin cotton gown didn't exactly give him leverage, for one thing.

"We didn't come here to argue," his mother said, her soft voice insistent, a little panicked. She hovered by Finn's side, checking his head. "How are you feeling?"

"I'm fine, Mom." Actually, his head was pounding, and his body ached like the last time he'd tried boxing, but it really wasn't the time to mention it. "If Dad hadn't hired the P.I.s again, you wouldn't have known about it until I was completely recovered. You wouldn't have had to worry."

"What's next, Finn?" his father said, pacing at the foot of Finn's bed like a lawyer prowling in front of a jury. "You going to start playing Russian roulette? Going to dive into a live volcano?"

"Well, in a few weeks I'm supposed to get shot out of a cannon," he said, remembering Ben's second challenge.

"That's not funny, goddamn it."

"It's my life, Dad. I know you don't approve, or agree, but it is my life."

"I could cut you off," his father said. "Kick you off the board, make sure you didn't draw any pay from the stocks."

"Dad, I don't touch the money you guys give me at this point." *For exactly this reason,* he thought. "I've still got the money from Grandma Macalister. And..." He looked at his mother, not wanting to remind her of his other source of income. "The other, you know, hospital money. So go ahead. Cut me off. Cut me out of the will, if you want."

"What difference would it make?" His father's eyes shone with anger. "At this rate, *I'm going to outlive you.*"

His mother let out a strangled sob.

"There. See what you've done?" his father bellowed.

"What *I've* done?" Finn protested.

"You don't even care that you're tearing your mother apart. Don't care about what this is doing to your mother and me!" His father's face was red, his voice deep, ringing through Finn's already-pounding head like a kettledrum. "When the hell are you going to grow up, Finn?"

Finn closed his eyes, wincing. "Why do you think that 'growing up' is doing whatever you tell me to do, Dad? How is that maturity?"

"And now you've joined some cult!"

Finn's eyes flew open at that. "I've *what?*"

"George told us," his father said, and Finn's stomach roiled. He'd have some choice words for his cousin when he got back to the mainland. "That…gamers club, whatever it's called. He said that they're adrenaline junkies. Says the police hate them."

Finn took a deep breath. "That's not right, and George knows it," he said sharply, wondering how to explain to them that since George had been expelled from the Club and the stupid, frat-styled pranks had stopped, the police really didn't have an issue with the Players anymore. And since George had personally screwed up by trying to get the police chief to shut down the Club, an act that had backfired spectacularly, the attention of the police had disappeared.

"I've read the newspaper articles about them," his mother interjected, taking Finn's hand and squeezing. "Oh, honey…I think…you might want to get help. If you need it, your father and I know some of the best treatment centers in the world. We can get you in tonight."

"Treatment?" Finn echoed, feeling more and more disconnected as the conversation grew more surreal. "Treatment for what? Adrenaline rehab?"

"Brainwashing," his father snapped. "They pull kids out of these cults. I'll just bet you've been reprogrammed."

Finn couldn't help it. He burst out laughing.

"Damn it, this is your *life* you're talking about," his father said. "And I'm not going to stop with just some lectures. You brought this on yourself, son." His father headed for the door. "Come on, Betty."

His mother gave his hand one final squeeze, then

leaned in to hug him. Then she leaned forward, kissing his cheek and whispering in his ear.

"How was your white count?"

Just like that, a spike of fear flooded him, until he took another deep breath. Pushed her question, and the past that prompted it, out of his mind.

"I'm *fine,* Mom," he reminded her firmly. "I'll talk to you soon."

TWELVE HOURS AFTER HER phone conversation with Thorn, Diana walked into the Four Seasons Oahu, dropping off all her luggage except for her attaché case, and asked to be directed to the Macalisters' suite. Her dove-gray business suit felt sticky and uncomfortable in the tropical heat, but fortunately she wouldn't be outside enough for it to bother her. She glanced out the window, looking at the impossibly beautiful blue sky, the waving palm trees.

Yeah, lucky you.

When she knocked on the hotel room door, Betty Macalister opened it, her pale face splotchy and wan beneath the remnants of expensive cosmetics. Everything about her seemed to scream *fragile,* from her delicately curled corn-silk blond hair to her watery blue eyes, to her translucent porcelain skin. "Diana?" she asked. "What on earth are you doing here? You can't expect Thorn to…to sign contracts and do business today!"

Diana kept her face impassive, especially when she saw her boss, Thorn. He was shaking his head slightly. "I told you I was sending for Diana, remember, hon?" he said, his voice calming.

Betty's expression of irritation melted into confusion. "Did you? I suppose... I'm sorry, Diana. It's been such a hard night, and..."

"Why don't you lie down. Take a sleeping pill," Thorn said, ushering his wife gently into the master bedroom. A few minutes later, Thorn stepped out, shutting the door quietly behind him. He looked at Diana with murder in his eyes.

Diana took a deep breath, then pulled a legal pad out of her case along with her mechanical pencil. She sat down at the dining room table. "What are we dealing with," she said, voice even, "and what do you need done by when?"

And who do you want murdered? Diana added silently.

Thorn kept pacing, and Diana waited. She knew how he worked, especially in a temper. Her boss would need to get rid of some emotion before he could logically come up with a plan of attack.

"I could kill him," Thorn said finally. "He's my only son and I love him, but for putting us through this, I swear to God..."

He choked off the words, slamming a palm down on the back of one of the high-backed dining room chairs. Diana had seen her boss in a fury before, but it was never comfortable. She wrote *Finn* at the top of the paper.

"He decided to surf the damned Banzai Pipeline. Waves the size of an 18-wheeler, for God's sake. Even experienced surfers get killed on it. But does that stop Finn? No. Of course not. He signs right the hell up."

It felt like a rant, Diana thought, as he shifted to a list of Finn's many past transgressions: running with the bulls, BASE jumping from Hoover Dam, trying to climb the Eiffel Tower. She remembered that one: negotiating with the French authorities had been a pain in the ass. If Betty hadn't been so upset, Diana would have been tempted to leave Finn in one of their five-by-five-foot cells for a few months, merely out of spite.

After what felt like hours, Diana fought the urge to glance at her cell phone to check the time. She understood that her boss needed to blow off steam, but when it came to family matters, he tended to use Diana as a sort of substitute shrink and sounding board. Which was fine, she reassured herself—she was more than just a lawyer to the Macalisters, she knew that.

Still, flying overnight just to hear about the sexy, spoiled Finn was pushing it, even for her boss.

"And now he's involved in some damned cult," Thorn growled.

Her attention snapped back like a rubber band. Cults often targeted rich kids—bled them dry, cut off all contact with families. She gripped the pencil tighter. "Which cult?"

"He's part of that…that thing. The Club." Thorn scowled, waving his hand as if she ought to know what he was referring to. "The Gamers' Club."

She tilted her head as her mind shifted gears. "You mean he plays Dungeons & Dragons? They are sort of dedicated, a little vehement. Maybe a bit nutty. But I don't know that I'd really call them a cult." She paused, reconsidered. "Not a dangerous one, anyway."

"No, no. The Player's Club," he corrected himself. "That's it."

Now her eyes widened. That made a lot more sense. The Player's Club was an urban legend in San Francisco—everybody knew someone who knew someone that claimed to be in it, but very few had ever *met* anyone who really was. A reporter had gone so far as to try undercover research to write about them. The story played up the Club's image of a notorious, underground group of thrill-seekers who apparently pulled pranks and ran crazy antics all around the globe. The Players seemed like a mix of *Fight Club* and *Jackass,* only for millionaires. She remembered thinking they were a bunch of rich-kid adrenaline junkies.

Which basically described Finn to a T. "How did you find out?"

"George told me."

"George told you," Diana repeated, making sure that doubt colored her words. She knew better than to challenge her boss's perception—Thorn wasn't a fan of subordinates confronting him—but she wanted to say: *You're trusting your feckless, conniving nephew George, the leering, kiss-ass weasel?*

Thorn got the hint, and still frowned angrily. "I know George was in a bit of trouble a while back," he said. "But he and Finn used to be very close...especially when George was in college. Finn admired him, almost worshipped him, in fact."

Which would also explain a lot of Finn's problems, but no way was she hinting at that one.

"Right now, George is having a disagreement with

his parents, and my brother-in-law is taking a hard line with him, although they won't tell me why. All I know is, George asked me for a job, hat in hand. His boss tells me he's working very hard. Which is more than I can say for my son."

Diana squelched the sigh. Thorn's disappointment in Finn's lack of interest in the business would cue a different long-running rant, and one that would definitely absorb another hour of her life. "So George says he's a member of this Club," she said, writing down *Player's Club* on her pad. "What do you need me to do, Thorn?"

Thorn's eyebrows jumped up. "Get Finn out of it, of course!"

She let out a quick snort of laughter before she could stop herself. "You want me to find a supersecret, near-mythical underground club of rich kids, and get your son—who won't listen to anything his own family says—out of it. The son who routinely loses any private investigators you've hired to follow him."

Thorn's green eyes flashed. "By any means necessary," he spat. "Unlimited budget, and do whatever you have to. But he's out of that damned Club before they kill him!"

"Ah." Diana nodded, her mind processing even as her heart sank. "All right, guidelines. Do you want him kidnapped and taken to a reprogramming center? Or simply impressed by an outside threat that joining the Club is not in the best interest of his future health?" She frowned. "I think I've got a couple of people who could ensure that he did exactly what he needed to, with no permanent physical damage."

She was jotting those down as possible solutions when she glanced up and saw Thorn staring at her openmouthed. "Are you serious?"

"You said by any means necessary," she reminded him.

"I didn't say kidnap my son!" Thorn blurted. "And I certainly didn't suggest, what, hiring thugs to rough him up!"

She didn't smile as she crossed those options off her list. They'd served their purpose—showing her boss that he was being irrational. "I don't see that there are a lot of other choices here," she said. "I'll do some brainstorming, but I—"

"You'd really do those things, though. Wouldn't you?"

She shrugged. She hadn't been lying necessarily. As she'd grown up, her family had been involved in drug dealing and various other criminal pursuits, and she knew people who would happily break somebody's legs just to get a few Benjamins. But she also knew that Thorn, infuriating hard-ass that he could be, was not a jerk. In a lot of ways, he was a soft touch. It was one of the main reasons she'd put up with his high-handed behavior from time to time.

"Damn. You *are* the Hammer, aren't you?" Thorn's expression gleamed with pride, and for a second, she sat straighter, smiling back, basking in his admiration. "They thought I was crazy, promoting a thirty-year-old to lead counsel. But in the past five years, you've proven yourself tougher than all my other employees and most of my competitors. If I told you to blow up a mountain, you'd probably ask for a time frame."

"And a cost analysis," she added dryly.

"You know, I never did ask how you got those pictures on the guy who was trying to extort money from me," Thorn said, his voice leading.

She fell silent.

After a few minutes, Thorn gave in. "Fine. Don't tell me." He shook his head. "But I'm serious, Diana. Short of kidnapping him and roughing him up, I want my son out of this Player's Club before his luck runs out and he winds up dead. He doesn't see how it's tearing his mother apart, but I'll be damned if he keeps it up one more year. So you pull some of your ruthless magic, and make my boy straighten out."

Diana nodded. "I'll do my best."

"No," Thorn said. "You'll get it done. Period."

Which she'd basically said, she thought, but let him put his foot down. "Where is Finn now?" she asked.

"He's still at the hospital."

"I'll talk to him, see if maybe he'll just make this easy for me," she said, tucking the pad back into her briefcase.

"It's Finn," Thorn said, with a dry, humorless laugh. "How likely will that be?"

"Not likely at all," she admitted, straightening. "But I've got to start somewhere."

"MR. MACALISTER, WHERE DO you think you're going?" The nurse in the faded sea-foam green uniform demanded of Finn.

"All I have is a concussion and a boatload of bruises, so I think I'm going to rest someplace a little more comfy," he said, winking at the woman. He immediately wished he hadn't—the resulting thumping in his head was like the world's worst hangover. "Not that you haven't been a ray of sunshine, but if I'm going to be in Hawaii, I'd rather be somewhere near the beach. Now, could you be a love and get my…ah, there're my clothes."

"I'm going to talk to the doctor," the nurse muttered ominously, and left.

"Knock yourself out," he replied, and stripped out of his hospital gown, groaning slightly. He had his back to the door, so he didn't notice anyone stepping in until he heard her voice.

"Finn, I need to talk to you…."

He spun—another bad idea—and missed grabbing the bunched dressing gown at his feet. "Um, hello? Knocking?"

Then he got a good look, and he broke into the first real smile since he'd landed in the hospital.

Diana Song, just as cool and collected as she always was, in a pale gray suit with a crisp white blouse. Her black hair was done up in one of those twist things, not a wisp out of place. Her onyx eyes were wide as she took in his nudity.

She never seemed surprised, he noticed, and his smile stretched as he saw her staring at him naked, obviously trying *not* to look below the waist—and, equally obviously, failing miserably.

"See anything you like?" He wiggled his hips a

little, pain be damned. He was going to celebrate this moment.

He couldn't help but notice that she swallowed hard, just before her face turned into the expressionless mask she typically wore.

"That's some bruising you're developing," she said, softly. "You'll end up looking like a patchwork quilt."

He kept smiling, and reached for the gown. "You should see me when—"

"You've got to quit the Player's Club."

He felt the weight of the shock, and realized she wasn't there to give him flowers and flirt. If Diana Song was anything, it was the job. Still, he forced a grin, refusing to let her see she'd shaken him.

"What Club?"

She crossed her arms, staring at him impatiently. He stared back.

After a few long, silent minutes, she nodded at him—and for no reason that he could understand, she looked impressed. She also decided to take a different tack. "Surfing the Pipeline. That's not brave, that's stupid. You know that, right?"

"Seemed like a good idea at the time."

"Don't they all," she murmured. "Your parents are concerned that your next bright idea might be your last, and they're concerned that your involvement in this Club might be contributing to the quality and quantity of your well-being in a negative way...these excursions in extreme brainstorming, shall we say, have to end now."

"Those are some big lawyerly sounding phrases

there," he answered. "Intelligent girls are soooo sexy." Which was true, actually, but he mostly said it to annoy her.

If she was annoyed, it didn't show. "Your father has asked me to persuade you to see the error of your ways and choose a less-dangerous group of enthusiasts to join."

"Again with the sexy intelligence. I'm notoriously bad at being reasoned with. Ask anybody. I'm not the type to listen to logic." He repositioned his gown, giving her a slow once-over with his eyes. "No, I'm sure your best shot would have to be manipulating me with seduction and your feminine wiles."

"Duly noted. I was thinking more along the lines of lead-pipe cruelty, but it just goes to show that there are several avenues we can explore to achieve the desired results."

He suddenly wished he had his clothes on. Even though he'd been joking about her seducing him—sort of—it was tough to match wits when you weren't wearing pants.

"No offense, Diana, but you're the family lawyer," he said. "You're brilliant, but at the end of the day, what can you really do to me? Write me a strongly worded memo? Subpoena me within an inch of my life?" He leaned close to her, whispering conspiratorially. "Good God…are you going to *sue me to death?*"

He saw it—just for a split second, the way those sexy pillowy lips of hers curved into an unwilling smile.

"Come on, you know you wanted to laugh," he coaxed, wanting to see what she was like when she wasn't all buttoned-up in business mode. "That was a good one."

"How you missed your calling as a stand-up, I'll never know. Perhaps you could quit the Player's Club and pursue that instead."

"I'm unappreciated, it's true," Finn said easily. "But seriously, what does my father expect you to do?"

"Whatever's necessary to get the job done." Her voice, though low, rang like a hammer on a steel blade, strong, true and somewhat ominous.

With anyone else, that sentence would've been a meaningless platitude, like *there's no* I *in* teamwork, or *we give a hundred and ten percent!* But with Diana, there was something else. She'd put up with his father's insane expectations for years, and had been able to survive in a corporate environment where lawyers were as disposable as toilet paper, and treated very similarly.

That meant that Diana was tough. Driven. Probably not to be messed with.

Which meant, perversely, that he now *had* to mess with her. He really had no choice.

"You're going to stop me, then," Finn mused. "No matter what."

"Yes," she said. "Yes, I am."

He couldn't help himself. He let go of the dressing gown and stood, naked, crossing his arms over his chest and looking at her sternly.

"Are you threatening me, Ms. Song?"

She stared into his eyes, as still as a statue. "Are you trying to impress me, Mr. Macalister?" she countered. "Or perhaps going for another cheap laugh?"

He chuckled. "Now *that* was just cold." He stuck his tongue out at her, then turned, to tug on his shorts.

He'd miscalculated. His muscles screamed at him, and he grimaced at the pain. "Damn it." His shorts caught on his thighs. This was getting awkward. He looked at her. "I don't suppose you can help with this? I'm a little injured, here."

She sighed deeply, but walked over to him, putting her hands on his waistband.

"This is so odd," he remarked, trying to feel less helpless by joking. "Normally, most women would be trying to get these off."

"I'll just bet," she responded, and tugged the pants up the rest of the way, to his waist. "But I'm not most women."

He stopped her, putting his hands lightly on her forearms, keeping her close to him.

She was beautiful, he thought. A mix of Amerasian, Chinese, maybe a little Hispanic. Her eyes were deep brown, so dark they were almost black, and her hair black and glossy. Her cheekbones were high, her eyes almond shaped, her lips like plump, luscious raspberries.

Her expression was as determined as a Sherman tank.

"Sorry," he said. "I'm not trying to be a jackass, here. I tend to joke when I'm feeling boxed in. You were trying to show me who's boss, and that sort of thing inevitably makes me want to push buttons. Still, the naked thing—" he shook his head "—was inappropriate, and I apologize."

She looked surprised. Then she smiled.

"It's okay," she said, her voice warming. "It could've been worse."

He paused a beat. "So it'd be wildly inappropriate for me to ask you out to dinner, wouldn't it?"

"Finn, did you hear a word I said?" she said quietly. "Your dad's given me a direct order to get you out of the Player's Club."

"You'll still need to *eat,* though, right?"

She laughed. He liked the sound of it—low and rich, like a brush of mink against his skin. "My job is to make you quit the Club…and from what I've seen, you're not going to just go along with it. So I'm probably going to be making your life a living hell until you do what I need you to do."

He grinned. "You'll try, anyway. But I've got some skills." He winked again. "So you do your best, and we'll see who wins."

"I don't play games," she murmured, but he could see it, the light of battle in her eyes. The challenge.

He felt his heart rev for a second, his body tingling, just like it did when…

He smiled as awareness hit him.

Just like it did before his favorite challenges.

"I'll be seeing you, Finn," she promised, then she walked away, her determined stride still ruthlessly sexy.

"I sure hope so," he said. "Let the games begin."

3

TWO DAYS AND three thousand miles later, Diana thought with disgust, and her stomach danced nervously whenever she so much as thought of Finn…and considering Finn had become her topmost priority, she couldn't help but think of him often.

It would help if you didn't think about him naked, though.

She closed her eyes, resisting the urge to put her head down on the steering wheel of her BMW. She needed to have sex. Why else would she be so distracted by a superhot, superrich, superspoiled pretty boy, who had never worked a day in his life?

Without warning, a vision of him, nude, his body cut like a Greek sculpture, popped to the forefront of her mind, and her whole body flushed with desire.

Yeah, why would you be attracted to that?

She got out of her car and slammed the door with unnecessary force. Even if her current task was to ruin his fun-filled life, he wasn't her type.

And God knew, she wasn't *his* type. Although she

wasn't quite sure what that type was, now that she thought about it.

And he was Thorn's *son.*

And he was five years younger than her.

And it was utterly, completely impossible.

Whatever the reason was, there was no chance of acting out any of the fantasies currently sneaking their way into her subconscious, so she needed to nip this attraction in the bud. Immediately.

Now that you've eliminated all hope of ever getting that hottie in bed, why don't we try focusing on the matter at hand?

By the time she made her way along the hallways of Macalister Enterprises, she felt more in charge, more herself. Quickly, she navigated through the maze of cubicles on the second floor to a small office in the marketing department.

Before she could figure out a plan to deal with Finn, she had to know more facts. She needed to start from the beginning.

Diana bypassed the departmental assistant outside George Macalister's office and went right to the source. George was chatting away on a cell phone. When he noticed her, he sent her a leering smile. "I'll call you back," he told whoever was on the phone with him, then he clicked the phone shut. "Well, well. If it isn't the Hammer. I haven't done anything that merits a visit from my uncle's enforcer, have I?"

What a goof. She smiled politely, then closed the door behind her, even though it was a bit like sitting in a walk-in closet. Despite the nepotism, obviously Thorn had intended George to start at the bottom, or close to it.

"I need to talk to you privately," she began, only to have him interrupt.

"How privately are we talking?" He leaned forward.

She ignored the innuendo and sat down in his guest chair. "I need to know how you found out Finn is in the Player's Club."

His eyes widened, then he shrugged. Nervous, she noted, and wondered if perhaps he wasn't making the whole thing up to try to discredit Finn. She'd heard that the two cousins used to be close, but in the eight years total she'd been with Macalister Enterprises, she'd never witnessed anything that suggested it. Of course, she tried not to keep track of the young Macalisters as the older ones kept her busy enough.

"I know because for a while we were both involved in the Club."

Her eyebrows went up a fraction. "Really."

He scowled. "What, you don't believe me?"

"Why don't you convince me," she said, instead, then held up a hand when he looked ready to launch into another one of his lame sexual references. "Tell me everything you can about the Club, give me any type of information or proof you have."

"We were all sworn to secrecy."

"That's touching," she said. "And yet, I don't care. What proof do you have?"

"I don't have, like, photos or anything," he protested. "I almost had video, but the bastards—including

Finn—broke into my house and took it. He *helped* them."

"I'd heard your house was broken into and that you were getting help from the chief of police," Diana said. "So if you know who broke into your house, why isn't Finn under arrest?"

She crossed her arms. She was one of the Macalister family lawyers, in fact, she was head counsel. She knew when things were going on. The fact that George had done something to get the chief of police mad at him had not escaped her attention—nor the fact that George's family had sold the sumptuous house George once used to live in, which meant they'd essentially kicked him out. The breaking and entering charge had been dropped hastily.

If George thought he could manipulate her, he was even dumber than he looked.

George reddened. With his pale skin and red hair, the flush was unattractive. "I didn't have enough proof."

"Ah. Well, I'm not the police, George. I don't need to make a case for the prosecution."

"What *do* you need?"

"I need to get Finn out of the Club," she said. "If that doesn't work, then I could just make sure the thing is out of commission. No Club, no Finn problems. So why don't you tell me what you *do* have, and I'll go do my job. All right?"

He looked to be concentrating on something.

A thought occurred to her. "George, are you afraid that somebody in this club might hurt you?" Wow, what *had* Finn gotten into? "If you break your silence?"

She saw the incredulousness on his face and, a split second later, it evaporated. Putting on an overblown mask of concern, instead, he said, "Not scared, just... nervous. When I joined the Club, I thought it was going to be fun—parties, rowdy stuff. But the guy running it, Lincoln—he's got a past. Lots of secrets. He's a dictator, likes to be in charge, wants everybody to do things his way."

"Is he forcing Finn to do these dangerous challenges?"

"Are you kidding?" George said dismissively. "That's pure Finn. He's forcing *other* people to do stuff, more and more life threatening. He's taking the philosophy, and he's...*twisting* it." George was all but pleading with her. "I don't even know him anymore. I think...he might hurt himself. Or...someone else."

Her crap-ometer went into the red, and she sighed. George wasn't going to be winning an acting award anytime soon. He was trying to discredit Finn, pure and simple. Perhaps it was time to do a little research into George's activities, as well.

"Do you know where they meet? How many of them there are?" *Anything useful?*

"The meeting location changes all the time. There's about thirty members, but I got out with a lot of other people when Lincoln took over." His expression turned crafty, and he grabbed a piece of paper. "I can give you a few names, but that's the best I can do. Please, don't tell anyone I gave you this information."

"I'll be discreet," she said, forcing herself not to roll her eyes as he furtively handed her the folded paper.

She stood up, eager to get out of the cramped office and away from George. "If I have any further questions, I'll call."

"You know," he said, standing up, as well, "it's almost lunchtime. Maybe we could have something to eat. I could tell you about some of the adventures I had when I was a Player."

Ugh, gag. "I'm not hungry, and I have a ton of things to do today," she replied, keeping her voice neutral.

"Maybe some other time," he shifted the point easily. "Or how about dinner?"

"I don't date clients."

"I'm not your client," he countered, and got into her personal space.

She yanked open the door, shoving him a little with her elbow until he jumped away. "Technicalities. Keep up the good work, George."

George was up to something, she thought. Fortunately, he seemed to lack follow-through, and right now, he was the lesser of her problems. As she headed to her office, she opened the piece of paper George had handed her. There were only a few names, but the one he'd written at the bottom was underlined.

Lincoln Stone, she mused. She'd start with him.

GEORGE LEFT WORK EARLY, heading for his favorite hangout, a bar about ten minutes away from Macalister Enterprises—close enough, but not so close that he'd run into other people from work. He got his usual booth and his usual order—a dirty Stoli martini. Then he sat and waited.

Victor, one of the aspiring accountants toiling away beneath Macalister's chief financial officer, showed up, managing to look equal parts scared and irritated. He was tall, stick-thin, with mouse-brown hair and a receding hairline, somewhere in his early forties. "I got here as soon as I could," he said, slipping into the booth. "Couldn't we have met somewhere more private?"

"He's not trying to shag you, Victor," another voice said, low, with a distinct British accent. "Are you, George?"

George grinned, even as Victor looked uneasy when the newcomer, "Jonesy" St. James, neatly boxed him in on the other side of the booth.

"Just water for me," ordered Victor. George saw sweat beginning to bead on the man's forehead.

"Double Johnnie Walker Black, neat," Jonesy added, dismissing the waitress. "What's going on, George?"

"Diana Song came to see me today," he said, and was gratified to see Victor white as a ghost.

"What? *Why?*" Victor squeaked.

"Wait a minute," Jonesy interrupted. "Who's Diana Song?"

"She's the lead counsel for the family. Sort of like my uncle's *consigliore,* to use a mob expression," George said, leaning back against the upholstered seating. "She's also his fixer—the one who makes sure things run smoothly."

"She's onto us," Victor said, and quickly motioned for the waitress to return to their booth. "I'll have a Cosmo."

"You will *not,*" Jonesy said, with a laugh. "God,

man, have you no shame? Do you carry a purse, as well?"

"Relax, Victor," George said. "She was asking questions about the Player's Club. And here's the beauty part—Uncle seems to have assigned Finn to her."

Victor slumped, grabbing his new drink. "I still don't like it," he said. "Damn it, George, I thought I said stay under the radar. If you attract attention to yourself, you're going to screw this up!"

George bared his teeth, ready to chew the guy out, but Jonesy was quicker to reply. "Now, Vic," he admonished. While his voice remained low, there was a raw promise of violence in his demeanor. "A man would think you were the one giving the orders around here with that tone of voice."

Victor blanched and George simply smiled. Befriending Jonesy had been one of the best moves George had made since the whole debacle with the break-in and Juliana Mayfield's interference. After the bitch had given the chief of police the video of George enthusiastically screwing his daughter...well, the case against Juliana and her Player's Club buddies gaining access to his computer hadn't held up. George's parents were pissed enough to kick him out and cut him off, forcing him to beg for a job from Uncle Thorn. He'd had to move out of his mansion into a crappy town house.

He'd been drinking heavily and complaining to anyone who would listen and so, over the course of several martinis and some jovial conversation, he'd subsequently discovered Jonesy, his new best friend. Jonesy, like himself, had also been cut off from his parents' money, only he wasn't going to let a little thing like that stop him.

They'd gotten good and drunk, and when Jonesy had come up with the embezzlement plan and how easy it would be…well, things just started to fall into place.

"I'm just saying we have to be careful," Victor cautioned, draining his girlish red cocktail.

"Trust me. I know what I'm doing," George said, working on his second martini. He felt ebullient. Finn was going to be sorry. That was the bottom line. George was going to get revenge for getting kicked out of the Club and having his reputation damaged. "The plan was to get money. The embezzlement ought to work like a charm—they will find out, eventually, but I don't plan to be on the run forever, and frankly, we're not taking enough money to fund that. We only need to find a fall guy to pin this on."

Victor blinked. "That wasn't the plan!"

"He's right," Jonesy said, and George felt a little uneasy. "That wasn't the plan I gave you."

"Don't worry, you'll still get your cut," George assured him. "But if we can nudge the blame onto Finn… well, that'll free up the board seat, which means I'll have a steady, profitable income, and I won't have to do a damned thing. So money now, money later, and everybody's happy." *Except for Finn,* George thought. The idea of his smarmy cousin locked up for a while in Club Fed was enough to bring a smile to his face.

"It's not set up for a frame job," Jonesy said, his cultured tones shifting to something a bit more streetwise before he could catch himself. "The next time you improvise like this, you'd best warn me."

"How hard can it be?" George said, looking at Victor.

"Very hard!" Victor shot back.

George leaned in close. "Then I guess you'd better figure it out," he said softly, "because right now, it's all pointing at *you,* Victor."

Victor swallowed hard. Then he pulled out his wallet, dropping some bills on the table. "I've got to get back to the office," he said, then pushed past George and fled the bar.

"Gotta keep an eye on that one," Jonesy warned, shaking his head as George laughed and sat back down. "Don't know that I can trust a man who can order a Cosmo without a trace of embarrassment. He's the weak link, and he'd be quick to roll over."

"It's going to be fine," George said, although he wasn't convinced. "Besides, if push came to shove, Victor could just pop the money back and make it look like a big accounting error. That happens all the time."

Jonesy's expression went blank, his eyes flat and cold as a snake's. "No, mate," he said. "The money's not going back."

George blinked. "Well…no. I mean, it could, if there were problems. But there won't be any problems."

Jonesy did not seem comforted, so George plowed on.

"Besides, with Diana and my uncle distracted by Finn, they won't even start to investigate any discrepancies. They'll have their hands full with my cousin."

"You'd better hope so," Jonesy said, toasting him with his raised glass of whiskey. "Still, maybe I'd better look around, see if there's any way we can't tie off some loose ends while we're at it. Make sure this thing goes off without a hitch."

"Sure, sure," George said absently, motioning for his third martini. Diana wasn't going to be a problem. Finn wasn't going to be a problem. It was all going to go George's way, he thought. And about damned time, too.

4

IT HAD BEEN a frustrating week. It was nine o'clock at night and Diana was just driving away from the office. When her phone rang, she clicked on her Bluetooth headset. "Diana Song," she said, her words clipped.

"Di, we lost him."

She gripped the steering wheel so viciously she would be surprised if she didn't leave indentations. "Bob, you're one of the best private investigators ever," she said. "So could you please tell me why it's so hard to find one twenty-nine-year-old rich kid?"

"Anyone else, I'd say it was a walk in the park." Bob's nondistinctive voice, strangely enough, matched his completely average look. Which explained why he was one of the best private investigators in the business. "I don't know how he made me, or the two guys I subcontracted to. Kid picked 'em out right away, and trust me, it wasn't because they screwed up. I don't suppose you warned him that you were going to be following him?"

"No," she said, then frowned. "But I get the feeling his father might have inadvertently given him the heads-up. Damn."

"Won't be making my job any easier."

"So, up your rate," she said, pulling into her driveway. She parked the car, then took out her notepad to write *ask Thorn re: what he told Finn.* "You have no idea where he is now?"

"No." At least Bob sounded embarrassed.

"Well, he drives a flashy car," she muttered. "A Jag, I think. Maybe a Porsche. How hard can that be to spot?"

"That's the thing. He parked near Union Square, headed toward the public transit, got lost in the crowd and took a Muni."

"The bus?" She blinked. "Huh. I wouldn't have expected it."

"Trust me, neither did we. This is the third time he's lost us, and that chaps my ass. Kid is a shadow. If you're serious about finding this guy, I may have to use less than strictly legal means."

"We're not there yet," she murmured, "but you'll be the first one I call when we are. And I imagine that's not going to be cheap."

"You get what you pay for. In the meantime, how about I hire a few more guys to help me out. That's going to cost, too."

"Yeah, I know." She needed to figure out how to justify the overage to Thorn. He might say there was an unlimited budget, but the man still expected the moon for a penny. She knew her boss, and for all his millions, he watched money like a hawk.

That reminded her of another headache. One of their

accountants had emailed her about some discrepancies. As if she had time for one more thing on her plate.

"Hire the new guys, Bob. In fact, hire other new guys to check out whomever Finn meets. I want full workups on anybody he hangs out with." She paused. "And I want an in-depth investigation on this Lincoln Stone guy. Beyond the strictly legal, Bob," she said, with emphasis. "I'll sign off on the invoice myself."

Bob let out a low whistle. "Going to war, then, are we?"

"Just being prepared," she replied. "I'll keep an eye out for that report."

She ended the call, then closed her eyes. She needed to schedule a massage or something, she thought wearily. She was wound just a little too tight.

She got out of her car, headed for her front door, and as was the norm lately, her mind drifted back to Finn. Who knew he'd be such an escape artist?

As she got closer to her door, she realized something wasn't right; her stomach tightened, and that creepy feeling of being watched tickled at her senses. Struggling to appear casual, she reached into her attaché case and dramatically yanked out her mace, aiming it at the hydrangea bush next to her.

"Whoa there, easy now," Finn said. "I'm unarmed and defenseless." He came out from behind the bush, grinning, with his hands up.

"Unarmed maybe," she said. And pointedly didn't put the mace away. Her heart was pounding like a hammer against her sternum. She was still jumpy enough, and angry enough, to spray him just for the hell of it.

"I'm surprised you didn't know I was here." His hazel eyes twinkled. "I mean, you've got three really decent private investigators following me, right?"

"As far as you know." He was cocky. Why in the world would that provoke a smile? Irritated with herself, she put the mace away and walked past him, unlocking her front door. "You've proven you're smarter than my investigators. The trick's going to be proving it tomorrow or the day after that."

He followed her to her door, and her heart kept pounding even though she was pretty sure the adrenaline of being scared had worn off. "I like that about you. You're up for the challenge."

"I told you. I don't play games." She faced him.

He leaned in close enough that she could feel the heat from him like a tropical sun. "I do," he whispered, and she wet her lips in anticipation. "Play with me, Diana."

For a second, she wanted nothing more than to press her mouth against his. Mold her body against his. Drag him inside and see exactly what sort of games they could play.

"You're simply having a little fun here," she said, instead, angry at herself and her fantasies. "But I'm doing my job."

She turned on her heel, and yelped when he started to follow her again.

"What are you doing?"

"What does it look like? I'm coming in," he said. "It'll take twenty minutes for the cab I called to get here." His smile was so entreating, his dimples so charming, that it startled a laugh out of her. Why couldn't she stay mad at him?

"I didn't invite you here, and I certainly didn't invite you in," she told him, hating that she sounded breathless. What was she, in high school? She put on a stern frown. "If you've got to wait outside, that's your problem."

"Do you always take everything so seriously?"

She huffed out impatiently. "Do you take *anything* seriously?"

She'd made a fatal mistake, she realized. She'd gotten too close to him physically. Lost her stupid mind. She could smell his aftershave, something clean and male and vaguely outdoorsy. She could see the muscles that pulled his T-shirt taut against his chiseled chest. He seemed to sense her new appreciation, and moved forward.

"I take a few things very, very seriously," he replied, reaching out, touching her cheek, stroking gently. "I wouldn't mind showing you sometime."

"D-does that actually work on women?" she asked, trying for disdain and failing miserably.

"You tell me." His lips were just above hers, his voice caressing her. "Just tell me to stop, Diana, and I'll stop cold. But I have to say, I haven't met anyone who's intrigued me half as much as you."

"I'm not trying to intrigue you."

"Maybe that's why." His mouth…damn, she could all but *feel* it against hers.

She forced herself to pull away, breathing deeply. "Well, that's flattering. You're attracted because I'm not." She quirked up one of her eyebrows. "Don't they have a term for that sort of fixation? Like *stalker?*"

"I didn't say you weren't attracted." His eyes shone with amusement, and admiration. "I said you weren't trying to intrigue me, which is great, by the way. Most women I know figure out I have money and then do everything they can to hook me."

"I'm not trying to hook you," she said, insulted. "And I am not attracted to you."

"Liar." He drawled the word. If honey had a sound, his voice would be it.

She crossed her arms. "Okay. You've got me. I'm sooo attracted to you. Take me, take me now. Oh, baby." She rolled her eyes when he laughed. Damn. He had a great laugh.

"Now you're really hurting me." He backed off to her relief. "All I'm saying is, we're stuck in this situation. I know you're only doing your job, trying to get me out of the Club, and I'm not taking it personally. I hate it that my parents are spying on me and want to control my life. That said, at least this time they've put a gorgeous, intelligent woman on my case. I might as well make the best of a bad situation."

"When life gives you lemons?"

"Something like that." He winked at her. She didn't know anyone else who could wink and have it actually look rakish. "I guess it's a good thing you're not attracted to me, though. You do take things too seriously."

"Do I, now?" She frowned, feeling the same irritation she'd felt with Travis.

Finn shrugged. "I have a good time with women. We

have fun. But I get the feeling that you're not the type to just have fun." He shot her a quick, devilish grin. "I'd hate for you to kiss me, fall madly in love with me, then decide you couldn't live without me."

"And there's a danger of that?" she said, laughing at the sheer audacity of his tongue-in-cheek pronouncement.

"Unfortunately, yes," he said, and she noticed there was a glint in his eyes…something that suggested that, perhaps, there was a kernel of truth in his joke. "I'm a pretty good kisser."

"Thank God I'm made of sterner stuff," she countered. "Trust me, Finn. I'm not going to fall in love with you."

"You say that now," he muttered. "Heck, they all do."

That's when she knew that he meant it. "You honestly think that if I kissed you, I'd fall in love with you?"

"No. If you had sex with me, though, you probably would." He started to leave. "A kiss would probably mean you wouldn't stop calling me. I'll see you on the playing field, Diana. Or at least, I'll see *you.* Don't think your P.I.s will be…"

Before he could finish the sentence, before she could think the better of it, she'd grabbed him, turned him and kissed him hard on the mouth.

When she released him, he let out a chuckle. She barely registered it, just as she barely registered her shock at having done something so stupid. Something that, in a split second, *seemed* like a good idea…but really, really *wasn't.*

Then his chuckle stopped, they resumed their kiss, and just like that, her mind switched off.

She moaned softly at how amazingly good he felt. His hands circled around her waist as her fingers burrowed into the hair at the nape of his neck. His mouth was mobile and warm and oh, this man could kiss.

There was a faint honk, then another, a more impatient one. *If I don't stop now, I won't stop at all.*

Which meant she wouldn't be doing her job.

She always did her job.

She halted their kiss immediately. "That's your cab," she told him.

"Screw my cab," he said, leaning into her, and she gently nudged him back.

"I think I've proven that I'm safe from your charms, Finn," she said, striving for as cool a tone as possible. "So run along, before you get addicted to *me*."

Finn's eyes were wild; he seemed untameable. She trembled, her body screaming in protest as he took a step back. "This isn't over, Diana."

"Yes," she said, ignoring her body's reaction. "Yes, it is."

She shut the door in his face.

It was over. Because it had to be.

She found her cell phone, dialed Bob's number. "I'm working as fast as I can, Diana," he groused.

"Pull the trigger," she said.

Bob paused. "What, exactly, are you okaying?"

"I've got Finn's cell phone number. Track him." She closed her eyes. "Let's finish this. I'm through playing games."

THE NEXT NIGHT—MORNING, technically, since it was 1:00 a.m.—Finn was still grinning as he arrived at the Player's Club meeting. This time, it was at a bar down on the Lower Haight. It looked as if the decorator had been on an acid trip. There were weird sculptures from floor to ceiling, lava-lamp-style lights and trippy music, turned low to accommodate people talking. There were Club members showing pictures of their latest completed challenges—a few others in the planning stages for the next big Player's Club trip to Machu Picchu, or the next organized skydiving event. Three pledges made it through their challenges recently and were admitted to the Club, and now they were talking about bringing others in. There had to be at least sixty people in the after-hours bar.

"Glad you're okay, man," Ben, Finn's surfing pledge, said, clapping him on the shoulder. "Jeez, thought you were gonna *die* in the water there!"

He liked Ben, but he had to admit, the kid made him feel old sometimes.

"So." Ben rubbed his hands together. "The cannon shoot is in two weeks. Then...Everest!"

"Everest is like six months off," Finn pointed out. "Don't worry, we're okay stretching the deadline because it's such a huge challenge, but..."

Ben's eyes were gleaming. "Actually, I think we can pull off Everest in four weeks," he said, conspiratorially. "Six weeks, tops."

Finn blinked. "How the hell did you manage *that?*"

"Got some sherpas that are willing," Ben said. "If

you want it badly enough, you can do anything, you know?"

"That's great for your inspirational talk," Finn teased, "but...I don't know, maybe not for something like Everest."

"You're not chickening out, are you?"

Finn frowned. Any other time, he'd be right there with Ben. And while a part of him was clamoring, *Hell, yeah! Sign me up! Do this now, before it's too late.*

A new voice, surprisingly insistent, was asking, *What would Diana think?*

How the hell had she gotten into his head?

"Okay. Show me your plan, and if it looks all right, we'll go," Finn said.

Ben whooped, drawing the attention of a few Club members. Finn sent him off to get a drink and promptly found himself flanked by Lincoln and Juliana, as well as new Player recruits Scott and his girlfriend Amanda, and one of Finn's best friends, Tucker.

"Hi, guys," Finn said, then saw a matching look on all their faces. "Crap. What'd I do?"

"Ben," Lincoln said, nodding over at the kid who was now telling some enthusiastic story at the bar. "Great guy, very enthusiastic."

"You're getting shot out of a cannon." Juliana enunciated each word.

"You know, it turns out they don't use gunpowder," Finn offered. "It's a catapult, and they add some flash powder and a loud boom so it *seems* like a cannon. So it's not half as hard-core as you think it is."

"Really?" Tucker said, sounding disappointed. "That

sucks! What a rip-off!" When the rest of the group stared disapprovingly at him, he winced. "I mean… um…"

Finn grinned.

Lincoln studied him expectantly. "We still need to talk about Everest, Finn. Unless you were planning on faking *that* by just taking a hike through Yellowstone or something."

"How did you hear?" Finn quipped.

Lincoln glared at him.

"It's not my fault he's found sherpas who are willing to go up sooner than we'd planned," Finn protested. "And I'll go over every inch of his plan and make sure everything's safe before I— You didn't know about that, did you?" He felt stupid, as anger had lit up Lincoln's face. Juliana rolled her eyes, and the rest of them seemed stunned.

"Earlier than six months?"

Finn grimaced. "I'll make sure it's okay, Lincoln."

"I can't sign off on this," Lincoln said between clenched teeth. It was one of the rare occasions when Finn saw his best friend both pissed and frazzled. "We've said no to less-dangerous stunts."

"*You've* said no," Finn retorted, then felt childish.

"You'd say yes to anything, Finn." Lincoln didn't sound angry, merely sad. Maybe even disappointed. It rankled the hell out of Finn.

"You make it sound like I have a death wish!"

He expected some laughter or something, but suddenly, the crew was staring at him. Pointedly. Tucker even shot him a look: *Duh, dude. Why do you think we're worried?*

"Holy crap," Finn said, figuring it out finally. "I don't have a death wish. I *don't*."

"I'm just saying we can't approve this challenge," Lincoln said.

"What, you're going to kick Ben and me out of the Club?" Finn laughed, but then stopped abruptly, seeing the look on his friend's face.

"I think that maybe Ben might need a different mentor," Lincoln said, in a low voice.

"I brought him in." Finn felt insulted. "He barely knows anybody else here."

"He barely knows you," Lincoln pointed out, nodding at Ben, who was in the middle of an animated conversation with five other people. "And somehow, I think he'll manage."

"Listen, Linc, either you trust me, or you don't. What kind of friend are you?"

Lincoln's eyes widened.

"Time out," Juliana interrupted. "Go to your separate corners. Baby, Lincoln, get me a drink, please?" Without checking to see if he'd agree to it, she looped arms with Finn and dragged him off to a corner. "We care about you. Lincoln loves you, in that bromance, guy-buddy sort of way. You're his family, Finn," she said emphatically. "His only family."

"Guilting me isn't going to change anything," Finn said. "I've been guilted by the best."

"You are so stubborn." She poked him in the ribs, and he glared at her. "Lincoln's not going to just stand there cheering when the closest thing he has to a brother decides to get himself killed."

"I'm *not* going to get…"

A commotion nearby abruptly stopped their conversation. Finn saw seven men dressed similarly in dark suits. They looked like the secret service. Despite the bouncer's insistence that it was a private party, they remained where they were, until the lead guy's attention fell on Finn. With long, purposeful strides, he stepped right up to Finn and handed him a large manila envelope. "From Diana Song," he said, in a clear voice that carried. "She said to deliver this to you immediately, and that you'd know what to do from here."

Finn stared at him in disbelief. Then he burst into laughter. "*Seriously?* Okay, I am impressed. How did you find me?"

The guy shrugged. "You can ask her that. Excuse us." He nodded at Lincoln. The men filed out.

"What was *that?*" Juliana asked, noticeably shocked.

"That's just my family…" Finn answered, chuckling as Lincoln walked up to them, handing a drink to Juliana.

"Something I should know about, Finn?" Lincoln asked with a hint of cold skepticism.

"She's better than I thought," Finn mused, opening the envelope. Yeah, she was a hell of a challenge. He'd never even sensed a tail. Ms. Diana Song was turning out to be the most fun he'd had in…

He stopped abruptly as he saw the documents. Pictures…not of himself.

Of Lincoln.

And some bank statements, with a note attached, in what he assumed was Diana's neat, precise handwriting.

> It seems your friend Lincoln is head of the Player's Club…and he also seems to be laundering money. I imagine more incriminating or at the very least embarrassing details could emerge with even more effort.
>
> Perhaps it would be best if you quit the Club before the press finds out.

5

DIANA WAS JERKED OUT OF a deep sleep. Someone was pounding on her front door. She sat bolt upright, her heart pounding.

Police raid? she wondered, then remembered—she wasn't living with her junkie mother, wasn't living with a bunch of criminals anymore. Grabbing her bat and her mace, she headed for the front door.

"Damn it, Diana, open up!"

Finn. She should have expected this. He had all the impulse control of a three-year-old: if he got the envelope tonight, she shouldn't have expected him to confront her in the morning. She put down the bat but kept the mace as she opened the door. "Keep it down," she ordered. "This is a quiet neighborhood. You don't want them to call the police, do you?"

Then she stopped. She'd gotten a good look at his face. The normally unflappable Finn Macalister looked…dangerous.

"You had no right," he said, his voice reflecting fury.

"*No right* to look up Lincoln's financial details. You crossed the line."

"One I'd wager your friend has already crossed, in one way or another." She shut the door once Finn stepped inside.

"You couldn't have gotten that info by legal means," he bit out, glaring at her. "You broke the law."

"And you're all of a sudden a monument to the legal system? Organizer of the naked 5k through Golden Gate Park? Alleged coconspirator behind the Mighty Mouse Mural?" She pursed her lips. "Hello, Kettle? This is Pot, line one."

"I don't break the law to hurt people." He was in her space, in her face...his muscles bulging, his handsome face a chaotic mix of rage and pain and confusion. "And I never thought that you, of all people, would either break the law or hurt somebody innocent just to get what you want."

"His innocence is debatable. Still, the fact is, I told you. I *warned* you, Finn. But, no, you just thought the whole thing was a game. Worse, you thought it was a *joke*."

"And you thought it was a contract hit," he spat back. He loomed over her, his eyes blazing. "How far would you go to get me out of this Club?"

"As far as it takes," she snapped, retaliating. "You're mixed up with somebody who's laundering money. I've seen records wiped before. He must have paid someone to do it. What the hell have you gotten yourself involved in, Finn?"

"He's not... You don't understand!" He ran his hands

through his hair, a gesture of pure frustration. "It's not what it looks like, not what you think. Lincoln's clean."

"Maybe now," she guessed, and from the way Finn's gaze shot to her, she'd bet she guessed right. "Yeah. So he's got this little cult, a bunch of rich people, how convenient. How much is he bleeding you for a year, Finn? Or does he have you call them dues?"

"You're the snoop here," he said. "Why don't you tell me? You didn't look into my bank account?"

"Didn't have to," she said. "And I won't, if I don't have to."

"You mean you won't if I play ball."

She shrugged.

He took a few deep breaths, backed away from her, pacing in her foyer like a newly captured jaguar. He looked sexy like this: righteous, angry, so full of passion.

She could only imagine what that would look like—would feel like—if he weren't also looking so trapped.

"You can have my bank account. You can search my damned house. I'll submit to blood tests. But you've got to leave Lincoln alone. He's my best friend." He frowned, pausing. "Lincoln's put his past behind him. It would kill him to have it exposed. I won't *let* it be exposed."

She'd had too much practice to let the emotion bleeding through her show, but the quick stab of pain she felt at seeing his loyalty had her questioning her tactics. "So, you'll quit the Club?"

"I could… I could say that I quit. It's not like the

Club has membership records. Who's to know, one way or another?"

"Do you really think your father won't be able to tell?"

Finn growled. "No. If I do anything, he'll blame the Club, and you'll drop Lincoln in it. Really, this has never been about the Club. You're telling me to give up anything that my parents consider dangerous, basically, everything that I feel makes my life worth living."

She stilled, considering his point. "I hadn't really thought about it like that." She figured if she shut the Club down, or Finn stayed away from it, it would be enough. But the way Finn had painted it...yes, she could definitely see his parents' motivation.

A neat trap.

No wonder her boss was so damned rich.

Now Finn was like a man walking to the guillotine. Pleading. Desperate. And at the same time...noble, somehow.

Damn.

"You don't understand," he said softly. "How can you understand why I need this? How could you possibly understand?"

She put a hand on his shoulder. She could feel the tension singing through him, like a drawn crossbow line. And she could tell he *meant* every word. This wasn't the tantrum of a spoiled rich brat. She couldn't even begin to describe him when he was like this.

Why would a stupid club, or some life-threatening stunts, put a look like this on a grown man's face? Or that tremor in his voice?

"Maybe you could explain it to me," she heard herself say, surprisingly.

His voice sounded hollow. "Why would you care?"

"I don't care," she answered, then winced. Technically, he was just a task on her to-do list. He was her boss's son, and for a million reasons, completely off-limits.

So why did his pain pierce her this way?

"I shouldn't care," she whispered, correcting herself.

He took a deep breath. "The Player's Club isn't some playgroup for grown-ups. And we're not some pack of immature thugs, no matter what George tries to paint us as. It's a group of people who decided there's got to be more to life. People who are willing to look out at what they're afraid of, and what they dream of, and go after it."

"I believe you," she said.

For a second, there was hope behind his eyes, lighting him up like a comet. She wanted to bask in that light, in that feeling.

What does it feel like to hope like that?

"Diana," he breathed, but he didn't reach for her. Just stared at her, as if he were looking into her soul.

She was falling into his gaze. When he simply put a hand up, she couldn't explain why she suddenly felt compelled to step closer…to press herself against him, to rest her head on his shoulder. She knew now she was intoxicated by him.

Suddenly, she felt hotter than a thousand suns. Why, even the thin robe she was wearing felt too heavy. And why now, of all times, when she was about to snatch victory from the jaws of defeat.

She couldn't explain it and she couldn't fight it, either.

When he turned his head toward her, she turned to meet him, and closed the few short inches between safe and damned.

FINN HAD RIDDEN twenty-story roller coasters that threw him around less than the emotional ride he was experiencing with one Diana Song.

At the moment, with her full lips pressing against his, her lovely, lean body molding to him with only a thin silk robe as a barrier, well, he wasn't complaining.

When he had arrived at her door, he had been furious at her, ready to scream at her until she saw reason. The thought of her cold-blooded handling of Lincoln's life was enough to keep him at least a little sane, but there was something about her, something chemical, illegal, totally uncontrollable. The fact that she'd softened toward him only wrecked his righteous indignation.

And yet nothing had really changed. Diana would likely still be gunning for him, for Lincoln and the Club. So why, when she reached for him, did his body answer the call so enthusiastically?

Why the hell was he so hot for the woman who was, currently, his worst enemy?

He pressed harder; wanting to punish her with kisses. His mouth moved fierce and fast against hers. But it only seemed to flip a switch inside her. Her hands snaked up his chest to hold on to his shoulders.

He groaned as his body shuddered, his blood surging, his cock like steel. Conscious thought was a fleeing memory. His fingers were digging into her hips, starting to tug the hem of her short robe up high on her thighs. He stroked down, moving past the filmy material, to her stomach, toward her thigh.

She wasn't wearing underwear.

His cock strained.

She moaned, one leg brushing against his. Her nipples were like diamonds, poking against the slick black robe. She bit his lip, soft enough to be tempting, hard enough to know she meant business.

He tore himself away. "Bedroom."

Her dark eyes were dazed. "What?" She blinked a few times, rapidly.

"We move this to the bedroom," he said, nipping at the column of her throat and feeling her shiver against him, "or I swear I'll take you here."

He looked to her for a sign and got it. Her head shook slightly. "No," she said, but wouldn't look at him, so he wasn't sure if she was saying it to him, or to herself. "I can't. We can't."

She pushed him away, retreating. He could see the way the robe clung between her thighs, he could smell the scent of her arousal, mixing with the hypnotic scent of her...something spicy and exotic.

She still wouldn't look at him. She moved quickly, shaking slightly. "That was an aberration. A mistake. I promise you it won't happen again."

"Do I look like I mind?" he asked, grasping her hand. "Diana, look at me."

She finally did, and he was surprised to see a glassy sheen of tears.

"It's all right," he said, trying to sound soothing. "What's wrong?"

"You're the son of a client, and you're asking me that?" She rubbed at her eyes with the heels of her hands. "It's just...you're really cute, and hot, and there's...something about you, and I haven't had sex in like a year and a half and it's not really important. I'm babbling. I never babble." She frowned at him, as if it were somehow his fault.

"You don't want to turn in Lincoln," Finn said. "You don't want to kick me out of this Club."

"It doesn't matter what I want," she said, her voice slowly regaining her practiced businesslike tone. Her eyes still betrayed her sympathies, though. "What matters is what your father wants, Finn. I can't do anything about that."

"Just following orders, huh?" He couldn't help it; bitterness seeped through every syllable.

And with that, she closed off.

"What would we have here, Finn?" she asked, challenging him. She stalked to the far side of the foyer, surveying him the way he imagined she would a jury. Her eyes went low-lidded, and she smiled slowly. "We could have scorching sex. I bet you're a god in bed. I'll bet we'd probably have an unimaginable night...maybe even a few weeks."

Finn's body started to react, but he squelched the desire, even though his cock already ached.

The smile on her face was quickly replaced with a

look of…not exactly remorse. More like painful realism. The most painful realism he'd ever seen.

"But then, we'd be stuck with the fact that all we had was a few weeks' worth of sex. You'd continue butting heads with your father, and I'd be out of a job."

"My father wouldn't fire you for sleeping with me!" Finn said, then immediately realized—he'd probably fired lawyers for far less.

"Maybe not. But he'd fire me for not doing my job, no matter how unfair or criminal or wrong it seems."

Finn nodded, slowly. "Maybe…"

"Are you in love with me?"

Caught off guard by her question, he smiled sardonically. "I don't really know you that well."

"I don't know if I can love anyone," she said, cutting across his joking reply. "But I'll say this—I've always been able to count on the job. Until somebody comes along that seems more important, important enough for me to risk everything that makes me safe."

Dismissing him, she walked past him and opened the door.

"I'm doing my damned job."

6

DIANA WAS SANDY EYED and irritable. She'd spent the morning staring at the same accounting spreadsheet and gotten absolutely nowhere with it.

Finn, get out of my head!

She'd won; she had the leverage she needed to get Finn to quit the Club. She'd done the job. Goody for her, but working here, for Thorn Macalister, you didn't get the morning off for doing your job. You got more work.

Right now, that work was checking out why numbers in the general ledger were coming up screwy. She'd already flagged the comptroller to track a bunch of mystery codes, meanwhile some accountant or other was supposed to be looking at it—she had his name on her desk, Victor something. She started sifting through notes, then gave up after five fruitless minutes of searching. Her normally pristine desktop had been ravaged by a paper tornado.

It only went to show how crazy she was, if she'd let things get this disorganized.

Instinctively, she struggled to tidy, acknowledging

the headache that was brewing. The three ibuprofen she'd taken with breakfast had done nothing, probably thanks to the pot-of-coffee chaser she'd downed in an attempt to make herself more alert.

Finn probably talked to his father this morning.

"Not now," she said aloud, stacking papers into neat piles.

He probably told him he's giving up everything. Probably going to let the private investigators shadow him. Might even give up his passport.

"What Finn Macalister does is none of my business." She put away the folders in her file drawer with a sharp slam.

He probably hates you.

Just for a second, she rested her face in her hands. It shouldn't bother her. She didn't even know him.

It shouldn't tear her up like this.

"Diana? You okay?"

She quickly looked up, seeing her assistant, Penny, standing in her doorway, staring at her with concern. "Headache," Diana replied. "Too many numbers."

Penny smiled sympathetically. "Well, you'll get a break now. Big boss wants to see you, in the main conference room."

"Thorn wants me?" Diana asked. "Why? I emailed my report to him this morning." The Finn Report, she thought, stifling a sigh.

"Maybe he wants to congratulate you on a job well done?"

"Yeah. Maybe." Diana stood up, straightening her

suit. She wasn't convinced, though. It wasn't Thorn's style. Curious, she left her office.

The main conference room, next to the executive office that Thorn used, was called the marble room. An immense marble-topped table dominated the room. Imported from Italy, the conference table was like a sepulchre, huge and stately and vaguely creepy. The room was the ultimate home turf for Thorn—the place where he routinely pulled deals together and crushed opponents into dust. He didn't have any big meetings that she was aware of, she thought nervously. Or was she so off this morning, she'd somehow forgotten one?

She took a bracing breath, then pushed the mahogany doors open. "Thorn, you asked to see..."

She stopped immediately.

Finn was there, incongruous in jeans and T-shirt, standing next to his father, who was wearing a three-thousand-dollar dark gray suit. Despite the disparity in their attire, they wore the same look of determination.

Oh, crap.

She didn't want to stare at Finn, but she couldn't seem to help herself.

He didn't seem to hate her, was her first thought. He wasn't quite smiling at her, either, but there was a gleam of mischievous devilry in his blue eyes.

Her body went unaccountably warm before her brain noted with irritation, *He's up to something.*

She didn't know why that cheered her up, but it did.

"First of all, I have to congratulate you, Diana. In less than one week, you managed to get Finn here to finally face his reckless ways." Thorn's laughter boomed as if he were some kind of mythical god of war. "I don't suppose you're going to tell me how you managed that?"

She saw Finn's surprise, a hint of gratitude, and she simply shook her head. "Thorn, as you've always told me, the important thing is getting the right results."

"True, true." Another thunderclap of laughter. "I guess they don't call you the Hammer for nothing!"

Diana squirmed.

"Well, Finn here wasn't too happy to do so, but he's come to me with a proposition, of sorts, and I have to say I'm intrigued." Thorn put an arm around Finn's shoulders, squeezed. "Actually, I'm surprised—he's got some of his old man's skills when it comes to negotiation. I knew you had it in you, son."

"Must be in the blood." Finn's responding smile was grim.

Diana felt her blood pressure spiking, her head throbbing like the bass line at a strip club. What *the hell* was going on here? "I see. So you've changed your mind, Thorn, about the Club and Finn's participation in it?" She was proud the question sounded so mild, even though she felt like strangling her mercurial boss.

"Absolutely not." Thorn released Finn. "I still think the Club is dangerous." There was a hint of steel in his voice that told her that while he might seem calm and jovial, whatever was going on between him and his son was definitely a deal of some sort. Which explained the marble room.

Diana's nerves tightened as she waited for the other shoe to drop.

"You may think the Club's dangerous." Finn's voice was a clear echo of his father's, carrying the same steely, unflinching strength. "But my father is at least going to let me argue my case, and prove that it isn't what everyone thinks it is."

Finn's intensity tugged at her, made her twitch. The frisson of excitement that danced over her nerve endings was a mere chemical reaction, she insisted. Could she help it if the combination of sexy rogue and determined purpose made an impact on her?

"So," she said, clearing her throat and her thoughts, "he's got a grace period?"

"Exactly. He's got one month to prove to me that this Club of his is as worthwhile and life-affirming an organization as he's making it out to be," Thorn explained.

"Great. Glad you got that straightened out." *God save me from boys and their bets,* she thought. She would never get the week back that she'd basically wasted, nor would she be able to get her weird reaction to Finn out of her head. *Damn.* "If you'll excuse me, there's some work that I—"

"I told him that he couldn't come up with some nonsense presentation," Thorn said, holding up a hand to effectively cut off her exit. "I know him. He'd invent some sugarcoated theatrical extravaganza that made it appear they rescue orphaned puppies from burning buildings. No, no, this will be firsthand, personal evidence."

Her mouth dropped open. *"You're joining the Player's Club?"*

What would the stockholders do if they found out

their stalwart president and CEO was running with the bulls? Spray painting murals? There would be a riot. The stock price would plummet. No wonder he wanted her in here; she had to either come up with a way around this idiocy or figure out a strategy to keep it absolutely secret.

Her mind was already racing with ideas when his laughter broke through her frantic plans. "That's ridiculous, Diana. There's no way I'd do any of that craziness."

She let out a long exhalation of relief.

"*You* are."

She blinked. "I'm…what?"

"You're going to go through all these high jinks Finn thinks are so life changing in a positive direction. You'll do the stupid challenges, get hazed, whatever."

"Why me?" she yelped, stunned.

"Because I trust your judgment," Thorn said quietly. "I trust you implicitly, and believe me, I don't say that to many people."

"Try *any* people," Finn tacked on, earning him a frown.

"A whole month?" Diana repeated. "No, sir. Respectfully—absolutely not."

Thorn glowered. "This isn't a request, Diana."

She winced, but pressed forward. "You've hired me to be legal counsel," she said. "You hired me to iron out problems. I fix things."

"Well, now I'm telling you to fix my son."

"Ouch." Finn shifted his weight, covering his crotch. "That sounds painful."

She ignored him. "You told me to get Finn out of the Club. I did that. I can still do that. So why are you bothering with this charade?"

Thorn looked pissed, but he didn't look away. "Finn, why don't you tell her why I'm making this deal?"

Finn cleared his throat, all joking fleeing his expression. "If you go through with this, and you don't understand why this is so important to me...if you don't see that it's actually beneficial to me, rather than destructive—" he swallowed visibly "—then I'll not only quit the Club, I'll go to every board meeting. I'll take a job here at Macalister Enterprises."

Aha. Diana felt her stomach drop. Finn knew his father, and he'd used the one lure Thorn would be completely unable to resist. Fantastic.

Finn stepped toward her, and her stomach jittered. "But you've got to play fair, Diana. I'm trusting you implicitly, and Dad's promised, too, that you'll be completely impartial."

She closed her eyes.

"So what do you say now, Diana?" Thorn asked.

What could I say? "Yes, of course."

"Great." When she opened her eyes, Finn was smiling at her, his eyes shining, his whole body almost pulsing with vitality. She thought he was about to hug her. No. He looked like he wanted to do more than hug her.

"First meeting's tonight," Finn announced. "And Dad said you get to focus on just this all month. I'll pick you up." He winked at her, then nodded to his father and left the conference room, whistling.

She waited until the door closed before she spoke to Thorn. "He trusts you."

The "smiling dad" face vanished, and Thorn's expression turned sharp. "Don't you?"

"I know you."

If a stalking lion chuckled, it would sound like Thorn's responding laugh. "One month," he said. "No matter what, Diana, end this thing. You know what the answer is. Just make him believe you're going through the motions."

"What if I think the Club really is life changing in a positive direction?" she heard herself ask.

"Diana," he said, and his voice was low, dangerous. "You know better."

This was too important to Thorn for her to screw it up. If she let his son slip away…

She felt nausea hit her.

Oh, yes. She knew better.

FINN FELT A LITTLE NERVOUS. It was early for a Player's meeting—only eleven o'clock at night. They'd chosen an airplane hangar in Alameda for the location, and only twenty or so of the members could show up since so many had been hanging out the night prior.

Maybe it was silly, Finn considered. It had started out as both a joke and a source of adventure—meeting at ungodly hours, ostensibly to hype the meetings, and just to have that secret-society feel. But they had a growing group and a set routine now: the new recruits, the challenges, talking about what adventures people wanted to go on and when. Maybe it was time to find something more permanent: a set time, a set place. He blinked. In all nine years—God, *nine* years already—that they'd been running the Club, he'd never really thought in terms of any "permanence" for what they were doing.

"Could we wrap this up quick?" his friend Scott drawled. "Some of us poor suckers have boring day jobs, Finn. We need sleep!"

Finn struggled not to make a face. *If I screw this up, I'm going to be one of those poor suckers.*

"Where are we?" Diana asked in an exasperated voice. She was leaning against him, which he liked; she was pissed as hell at him, which he was getting used to.

"New pledges are always blindfolded," he said. "Sort of a ritual to keep our meeting location secret in case a new recruit decides to back out. Speaking of secrecy, how the heck did your crew of spy wannabes find me before?"

She smiled. "Trade secret."

"You are one dangerous lady," he whispered into her ear. "Maybe I'll just have to torture it out of you." Doing so, he got a whiff of her perfume...subtly sexy, intriguing, mysterious. Much like the lady herself.

"Okay, enough fun," she said curtly, but he could've sworn he felt her shiver. "Are we there yet? Can we get on with this?"

He saw Lincoln glaring at him, motioning to him. "Soon. Could you just, ah, sit here?" He guided her to a folding chair. A number of people were muttering and nudging each other as they nodded to Diana's rigid figure.

"Another pledge, Finn?" his friend Tucker yelled. "You've already got your hands full with that daredevil Ben. What does this one want to do? Fly in space?"

"Maybe invade Canada," another person joked.

"After this year, I don't know if there's anything Finn hasn't done," a third Player joined in. Finn took the teasing good-naturedly. Lincoln's dark expression conveyed the opposite.

"What's she doing here?"

The truth was Finn's only option. "I texted…"

"You told me you had another pledge, and that we had to convene an emergency meeting. You neglected to tell me *why*. And I seem to remember we all agreed we weren't going to run another pledge until this group…" He paused. "Why do I even bother trying to tell you these things? You've made me the den mother of this damned Club, and it's beginning to piss me off."

"If you don't like that, then you'll hate this," Finn said, took a deep breath, then dived ahead. "She's my family's lawyer."

Lincoln looked completely baffled. "She's…what?"

"Lawyer," Finn continued, his palms actually sweating. Even when he'd climbed out on the top of the Transamerica building, his palms hadn't sweat.

He couldn't imagine what he'd be feeling if Lincoln ever found out that Diana had researched Lincoln's financials. It had taken years for Lincoln to even admit to Finn, his best friend, that he'd gotten a fortune from the father who had never claimed him publicly. Lincoln still chose to bury that association. And the money from his father's Swiss bank account, while not from criminal activity, would still throw Lincoln's life open to a world of scrutiny—and pain.

Finn was willing to risk a lot to keep his friend's past protected.

"I've, uh, cut a deal." And was hoping Lincoln would be able to figure out a way out of it, but first things first. "I really need her to have a good experience with all of this. She's super repressed, wound like a watch. We're about helping people live life to the fullest, basically, right? Following what they want, facing what they're afraid of? Like *Dead Poets Society* meets *The Bucket List*?"

"You know I hate that analogy," Lincoln muttered.

Finn pressed on. "If the Club could help anybody, it would help her. Actually…it sort of *has* to knock her socks off."

"We're not the Rotary Club or A.A.," Lincoln said. "What, exactly, did you deal?"

"If she gives us the thumbs-up, then my folks get off my back."

Lincoln's eyes narrowed suspiciously. "What if she doesn't give us the thumbs-up?"

"Well…I, ah, quit the Club." He swallowed hard.

"Seriously?" Lincoln's skepticism was clear. "And they're planning on having you prove that how, exactly?"

Trust Lincoln to get right to the heart of it. "By no longer doing anything they'd consider dangerous."

Lincoln's eyebrows jumped up, but otherwise he kept silent, expectant.

"And…I'd fulfill all my duties as a board member, including regular attendance, *and* take a job at my father's company," Finn finished.

Lincoln stared at him for a second. Then he glanced over at Diana. "And you're letting all this ride on *her?*"

"I'm still sitting here, you know," Diana said from across the room, causing several of the Players to roll their eyes and make dismissive comments.

"You'd better start buying some ties," Lincoln said, scoffing. "I don't know how you got suckered into this, but this has to be the stupidest bet you've ever made. Take off her blindfold, and let's get on with this."

Finn went to Diana and removed her blindfold. She blinked owlishly, then sneered at the assembled Players. "So far, Finn, I'm not impressed."

"Boooooo!" Tucker said. "Throw her back. She's not Player material!"

Finn quickly jumped in before that became the rallying cry. "Trust me, she's going to be giving this her all," he said, staring at her intently. "Won't you, Diana?"

Her chin went up. He was learning to love that little expression—which just went to show how truly insane he was. "Sure."

He nodded, running through the rules as most of the other Players ignored him. Then he got to the questions. "What are you most proud of?"

She frowned. "This is part of the initiation?"

"Yup."

"All right. I'm proud being lead counsel for Macalister Enterprises."

She sounded it. Hell, she sounded the same way most marines did talking about being in the corps. Her back was straight as a level.

"Okay. What scares you the most?"

She stiffened. "Nothing."

Tucker booed again. "Come on," Finn pressed. "Everybody's scared of something. What are you afraid of?"

She gritted her teeth visibly. "Gunfire."

He tilted his head. Something there, he thought, but didn't press. "Okay. If you had a month left to live, and let's say nearly unlimited resources…what would you want to do?"

She stared at him blankly. Then she shrugged. "I'd probably write up a standard operating manual."

"Huh?" He glanced over his shoulder, to find the rest of the Players staring at her.

"A standard operating manual," she repeated, then huffed. "You know, something that would explain everything I had going on, my routine, et cetera, for my job replacement."

"You've got a month left to live, and you'd write an operating manual?" he repeated, awed.

"Of course. I wouldn't leave the new lead counsel in the lurch," she told them, making it sound completely self-evident. *Obviously with one month to live, I'd write something for my successor. Who wouldn't?*

The Players were apparently too stunned to boo. "Good grief. What the hell else would you do?" Finn asked, repulsed. "No. Don't tell me. You'd draw up a will, make sure that everything was accounted for and make your own funeral arrangements."

He was screwed. He was *soooo* screwed, and not in a good way.

"Don't be silly," she said, surprising him. "I've already taken care of all that."

"You're, what, thirty, and you've made your own funeral arrangements?"

"Thirty-five, and cremation," she said stiffly. "Why would I want to purchase a plot of land for something I won't even enjoy using?"

"That's actually very sensible," Lincoln said, with obvious amusement.

Finn rubbed his palm over his face, appalled. "So… you'd write a manual. And that's it."

"Well, yes."

Finn looked over at Lincoln, then the rest of the Players. "Um…this is…" He struggled for the right word.

"Unprecedented?" Juliana supplied, tongue-in-cheek.

"At least she didn't say she'd steal anything," Lincoln murmured, kissing Juliana's neck. Then he looked at the rest of the Players. "Anybody else have any questions?"

To Finn's surprise, Amanda, one of the newest Players, approached Diana. She was a slender, almost elf-like woman, with silvery blond hair and a delicate face. She was smiling. "I think I've got this one, Finn."

Diana watched her, almost warily. "There aren't many women here, are there?"

"We're changing that," Amanda said, pulling up a folding chair of her own. "Actually, I'm glad to see you here." Like the classic good cop, she kept smiling. "So, there's nothing you wish you'd done, like when you were a kid? Nothing you would regret missing out on, if given the chance? Have you wanted to travel or anything?"

"I've traveled a lot for my job."

"I'll bet," Amanda noted shrewdly, "but have you seen anything outside the airport, hotel room, or conference room? Did you ever just...you know, wander around? Do anything for fun?"

Diana squirmed. "I'm not a huge 'fun' person."

"Okay, so travel, then," Amanda said, with a meaningful look at Finn. Finn shrugged. "Any place in particular?" Amanda pressed.

Diana seemed to stare into space for a second, and Finn wondered if she was falling asleep—she probably hadn't had much the night before. "You know," Diana finally mused, as if she'd forgotten everyone else were there and was only talking to Amanda, "I have kind of wanted to hang out in Paris. See the Louvre, have coffee in some café or something. The people there always look so...I don't know, sophisticated and artsy and mellow, without being annoying about it."

Amanda burst out laughing. "You'd love Paris. What about when you were a kid? Any place you wanted to see?"

Diana colored, and Finn found himself leaning forward, eager to hear what she was going to say.

"I've never been to..." She glanced around defensively. "Um, Disneyland. Not that it's a big deal, but I imagine that would've been fun. As a child. At some point."

"Great," Amanda said encouragingly, then looked at Finn. "Anywhere else?"

"Not really."

"Anything you wanted to do?" Finn tried again. "Hang glide? Parasail? Bungee jump, maybe?"

"God, no," Diana said. "Heights are *not* my thing. I'm more of a water girl, myself."

"Water," Finn repeated. "Huh."

"This little getting-to-know-you interview has been fun, and all," Diana said sarcastically. "But are there any other questions, or can we move on to the hazing aspect of this, or whatever you call it? I've got to go to the office in the morning, and I'm running on about three hours of sleep."

Finn looked at Lincoln.

"None of them are Everest," Lincoln replied. "But she's got her three."

"No way," Finn protested. "No way am I letting 'write an office manual' be one of her challenges."

"Wait," Diana interrupted. "Three what?"

"She's the one who said it," Lincoln countered, smiling wickedly. "Besides, maybe it'll help her, especially when she's on that long flight to Paris. And then to Disneyland."

"Wait! Paris? *Disneyland?*" she hollered, jumping out of her seat. "I can't just—"

"Fine, fine," Finn grumbled, then brightened. "But I'm still going to haze her."

"Um, Finn," Amanda interrupted. "I don't think—"

"Remember how Scott felt after he'd skydived?" Finn nodded when Amanda sent a slow, sexy smile over to Scott. "Trust me, I think a quick shot of adrenaline is exactly what the doctor ordered for Ms. Office Manual over here."

"Skydiving?" Diana repeated, going pale.

"No," Finn said, winking at her. "Something water. You'll love it."

She glared at him, then stomped out of the hangar. The retreating click of her heels sounded like machine gun fire.

"You're so screwed," Lincoln said, echoing Finn's own sentiment. "What really convinced you to make this stupid bet, anyway?"

Finn thought immediately of the envelope—of Diana's threat to send Lincoln's financial history to the authorities.

"It's not important," replied Finn, hoping that his lucky streak hadn't finally and dramatically run out.

PARIS. SKYDIVING. Disneyland, for God's sake.

Two days and one massive migraine later, Diana was at the Macalister company gym, at midnight, running on the treadmill as if she could somehow sprint away from the craziness that was the Player's Club.

She was the only one in the gym. The only one in the building, as far as she knew, other than the security guards. She didn't pull late nights as much as she used to, admittedly, especially during her first years proving herself as a lawyer at Macalister Enterprises. Now, however, she was closing out everything on her desk to take time out for a month's worth of traveling and those idiotic challenges.

As high a priority as Thorn was making of her going along with the charade, that weird little accounting hiccup wasn't going to solve itself, and if that Victor character told her one more time that he was working on it, she would squeeze his neck until his head popped off. She punched a button to speed up the treadmill.

Damn it. Damn it all.

She was the Hammer, wasn't she? She was the one who was supposed to have ice water in her veins. Yet something about Finn made her run hot, she admitted… which also made her admit how much that bothered her.

After five miles, she slowed down, got off the treadmill, still feeling tied in knots. She needed…something. A vacation. A massage.

A good sweaty roll in the hay.

She rubbed her towel over the back of her neck, puzzling over the exact date she'd last let any man have carnal knowledge of her. She thought maybe it was spring. Or was it fall?

It bothered her that she couldn't remember.

"You looked like The Terminator, there on the treadmill."

Her neck made a snapping sound as she whipped her head up, her heart pounding. When she saw it was Finn, she forced herself to rein in her surprise.

"Speak of the devil," she said in a calm tone of voice, even though her pulse was still racing. "I didn't expect to see you here, much less this late at night." She paused for a beat. "Stealing something?"

"Ouch," he said, coming to stand next to her. "I, on the other hand, am not at all shocked to find you here. And yeah, I was looking for you…so here I am."

He was wearing his usual jeans and T-shirt. She felt vulnerable, wearing only her low-riding sweats and running bra. She was normally wearing something far more professional, a skirt suit that seemed to act like a suit of armor. She took a liberal gulp of water from her bottle. "Okay, you found me. What do you want?"

He smiled, his eyes gleaming with humor, although his look sent heat through her from head to foot. Suddenly, she was grateful the gym was air-conditioned.

"You've avoided my calls," he said, in a low voice. He was standing close, too close. Was he doing it to make her uncomfortable?

"I've been busy." Her voice barely bobbled, and she prayed he didn't notice.

His grin suggested he had noticed. "I seem to remember your boss saying this was your top priority."

"My boss says a lot of things." She recalled the conversation they'd had after Finn had left the room. "He means a lot of other things, too. And no matter what he said, I'm not letting the ball drop on my real job to go running around with a bunch of trust-fund brats with more money than sense."

Finn's expression tightened, then he shrugged. "We'll see if you hold that same opinion once you've gone through the challenges."

"You just don't let up, do you?"

"Not when it's important to me," he said. "We need to talk."

She felt a little shiver of awareness. "I…I need a shower."

"I'll wait." He didn't touch her, but his smooth raw voice was like a caress. She shivered again, tried to blame the air-conditioning even as her body said *Hey, it's late, nobody's around….*

Oh, no. She needed to shut that thought down.

"I'll take your calls in the morning," she said, and cursed the fact that she sounded breathless. "Seriously, Finn. I promise. You should…you should go home. Or to the Club, or something."

He shot a quick glance at the treadmill, then at her. "What are you running from?"

"I'm not running from anything," she shot back, not realizing until then that she'd already made it halfway to the locker room. "I'm… I just… You confuse me, Finn. You're not really what I expected."

He smiled, and she felt another shiver. "I'm glad. Not just for the sake of the Club. I find you very, very interesting, Diana."

She flushed, noticing the way his T-shirt was pulled tightly across his body, the way his abs were ripped, and his shoulders…

Oh, yeah, you so need to have sex.

"Okay. Yes. I'm running," she muttered. "Good night, Finn."

She retreated to the women's locker room. She tried to collect her thoughts as she stripped out of her clothes.

The water in the shower was hot and pulsing, and utterly not helping.

She took the world's quickest shower, intent on getting home, although she still felt hot enough to melt a glacier. She turned the corner, only a towel wrapped around her body, and saw Finn.

She squeaked. "What the hell!"

"I'm sorry," he said. "But…I'm going to do this one thing, and then I'll leave. If you feel the need to beat the crap out of me, I will totally respect that, okay?"

"Wha—"

In a quick, fluid motion, he stepped forward, pressing his lips to hers.

It was like a brushfire. It seemed like the tiniest spark…and all of a sudden, the conflagration went up quicker than smoke. She should've been angrier. She should've been whipping out all her lawyer-ese on his ass, threatening him with jail time, sexual harassment, whatever. But she was too tired, too stirred up. Sensing her vulnerability, her body pulled a coup. Tonight, her hormones ruled.

She groaned, leaning into him, his hands surprisingly strong and weathered, gripping her upper arms. He backed her up against the nearest lockers. She felt her towel start to drop.

She didn't care.

He gasped against her mouth, his hands rubbed down her arms to her now-naked hips. He pulled her tight to him, and she could feel the delicious hard bulge straining against the fly of his jeans. She groaned again softly, stroking her pebble-hard nipples against the thin fabric of his T-shirt.

He pulled away only long enough to tug his shirt off, then he went to her. He threaded his fingers into her hair, pulling her against him so his mouth could plunder hers.

Yes, *plunder,* she felt invaded, but in the best possible way. Her body prepared for the onslaught.

She shoved aside any small whimpers from her logical mind—she'd deal with consequences tomorrow. Tonight, she was too ready and too damned hot. She needed this.

She was *taking* this.

Her hands slipped down his sexy, chiseled torso; she sought out and found the top button of his jeans. With quick movements, never breaking the kiss, she undid his pants. His erection was hard, velvety smooth and hot as an iron. She stroked him lovingly, shivering when he groaned against her lips.

"Diana," he rasped, leaving kisses on her chin, her cheek and her neck.

She couldn't wait another moment and shoved his jeans down past his hips.

"Diana, are you sure?"

"Don't ask," she said, and before either of them could think, she slung one knee over the hard, cut line of his hip. And watched his hazel eyes go dark with passion.

He lifted her, her legs wrapping easily around his waist. The cold metal lockers were a shock against her naked back, but in a second she didn't care. She wriggled, arching her back as he took one breast into his mouth, then switched his attention to the other. Now she was almost snarling with need.

"Please," she begged, barely coherent. "Inside me..."

He moved his hand between them, positioning himself, and she felt the blunt, broad tip of him. She almost wept with gratitude.

With one smooth, powerful glide, he thrust inside, and she spasmed, coming in an instant, letting out a low, shrill shriek.

"Did I hurt you?" he asked, his voice full of concern.

She was still clutching him, her body still tingling deliciously. "No," she said, leaning her head against his shoulder. "No, I just came."

"Really? I hope you don't think you're done with me." His low chuckle sent more pulses of heat from where they were joined, radiating out to every inch of her body.

She smiled. How could he make her feel like laughing at a time like this? "Yeah, I've got my ticket punched, I guess I can..."

He surged forward, making further speech impossible. She gripped his shoulders as he moved like a dancer, finding a sensuous, irresistible rhythm. A minute later, she felt her body start to climax again, felt the familiar anticipation working its way through her.

The rumors were true—Finn was a master. She felt like a plucked guitar string, vibrating, all but singing with the pleasure of it. She urged him deeper, her feet crossing at the small of his back as she ground against his spear-hard erection. Her breasts bounced and rubbed against his hard chest. He leaned down, kissing her as he held her, his cock moving swiftly in and out of her. She bit his neck and he jolted, hitting her just in the right spot. The friction, the rhythm, the pleasure…

The first orgasm had been like a gunshot. This was like an explosion. He pumped into her, forceful, and she loved it. Then he shuddered, collapsing against her, breathing ragged. He shifted her, cushioning her between himself and the wall of lockers.

"Amazing," he eventually croaked, after they both had caught their breath.

Right about then, with the primal part of her brain sex-sated and sleepy, the logical part got free…and mentally smacked her.

Oh, crap. She hadn't just made a mistake. She'd created a disaster.

7

"SHE'S ONTO US, I'M telling you." Victor spoke hoarsely. "We're screwed."

George chuckled. They were at Jonesy's place this time, a sweet penthouse, even if it was over in the Mission. "So Diana's been asking you some questions. She noticed some discrepancies. So what?"

"She understands accounting, which is more than I can say for you two," Victor spat out. He'd taken off his suit coat, and the armpits of his dress shirt were stained. The guy was a wreck. "She's going to put this together. We've got about a month to stop everything and fix this so nobody ever finds out. We've got to abort."

"Say, now," Jonesy said, coming from the kitchen and handing George a drink. "What's this? Nobody's stopping anything."

Victor's look of disgust was intense. "You're not the one with anything on the line, *Jonesy*. I don't even know what you're doing in this in the first place!"

Jonesy's smile was feral, and Victor shrank back.

"I'm the man with the plan, aren't I?" Jonesy took

a swig of his whiskey. "And the one with a calm head, it seems. Left to your devices, Vic, I don't think you could steal a pack of gum. How'd you get involved in all this, anyway?"

Victor risked a quick, ugly scowl at him.

George took a sip of his martini—dry as the Mojave, just the way he liked it. "Vic's got gambling debts, it turns out."

"Tsk, tsk. Nasty habit, that." Jonesy shook his head. "And I'll bet it'd be hard to keep a job at a place like Macalister, when word of *that* got out, eh?"

Victor's face turned beet-red. "You wouldn't dare!"

"Like you said, mate…not my ass on the line." Jonesy cheersed him with his drink. "Can I get you a Cosmo? Or…let's see, I have vodka and Gatorade, I think. Close enough—you look frightful."

Victor gritted his teeth.

George stepped in. "Why a month, Victor? What's going on?"

Victor shrugged. "I don't know. She's going on a vacation or something."

"A month-long vacation? That doesn't sound like Diana," George mused. "What, did someone die? Ha!"

"Hard to tell. The secretaries were gossiping about it." Victor's eyes danced a little. He seemed to be something of a gossip, himself. "All I know is, Finn's been calling her, and she's supposed to be doing some traveling. On the company, apparently."

"Really," George said. "Now, that's interesting."

"Is it?" Jonesy noted, sounding bored. "What does this have to do with anything?"

George ignored him, focusing on Victor as a twinge of nerves started quivering in his stomach. "Don't suppose the secretaries mentioned where she was going?"

"Penny, her assistant, said she got first-class tickets to Colorado, Anaheim and Paris."

Colorado? Anaheim? Paris?

He suddenly closed his eyes. "Wait a minute. You said that Finn was somehow involved? He's been calling her?"

"Yes. I figured he wanted her to bail him out of jail or pay off somebody, like usual," Victor said, with a shrug. "Penny says he's been flirting with her."

"Penny says that," Jonesy said, snorting. "You two sound like a silly sewing circle."

"No, this is good," George said, his mind beginning to rev like a Porsche engine with the needle in the red. "I think I know exactly where this is going, especially for an uptight workaholic. It's an uncharacteristic change.... I bet he's recruiting her. Damn it. And Uncle Thorn's letting him." George grinned.

"I hate to belabor this," Jonesy said with irritation, "but *so what?*"

"Uncle Thorn's trying to shut Finn down by having Diana go in undercover. So the old guy's finally hitting the end of his rope." George grinned. "That board position of Finn's is as good as mine."

Victor frowned. "If that's the case," he said slowly, "why has Thorn also approved remodeling a new executive office for Finn?"

George's revving brain spun out. "He's *what?*"

"He's having one of the big offices on the twenty-eighth cleaned and updated," Victor informed him. "And he's having business cards made up for Finn... put a rush on them, I saw the invoices. He wants everything ready by the end of the month."

George felt his pulse pounding, and couldn't contain his rage. "What the hell?"

"Still want to follow Vic's advice and tuck that money back where we got it, Georgie?" Jonesy said, with a cruel smile. "Still want to cruise on that nonexistent salary from the board member job you're not going to get?"

"No." George's hands formed into fists, and he broke the martini glass. Ignoring Jonesy's curses, he shook the remnants from his fingers. "We're going to ensure both Finn *and* Diana are cut out of this for good. Victor, here's what we'll do...."

FINN TOOK A DEEP BREATH, enjoying the clean, bracing air. He and Diana had taken the flight to Colorado, arrived at the river early that morning, and he'd set up their tents. In the distance the mountains looked like a postcard. Towering evergreens lined both banks of the nearby river. This was her first Player's Club event—her initiation, rather than one of her challenges—but he thought it would capture exactly what he'd always felt about the Club and taking chances. "You know, I love this," he said to Diana. "Why don't I come here more often? We should totally do a Club excursion here sometime soon."

"Whee."

He stared at her. She was wearing a neon orange

helmet and matching life jacket, and was holding her oar as if she were going into battle, he thought with a grin. She definitely looked like a samurai adventuress, full of grim determination.

At least she wasn't scared. He recalled one of their recent recruit's hazing. The guy hadn't liked heights, but he'd been so willing to change his life that he'd plunged out of the aircraft tethered to Finn. Finn could still remember when the guy's cursing stopped and he started whooping with glee.

It had changed his life, Finn acknowledged, barely noticing the increasingly choppy water up ahead. That guy, Scott, had since run with the bulls in Pamplona, climbed a pyramid at Machu Picchu, and was happier in his job and his life than he'd ever been. The fact that he was in love with a great woman, who was also now a Player, had only added to Scott's overall life change.

I'd like to see Diana feel that. In fact, he'd settle for simply, purely *happy.* He didn't think he'd ever seen an expression that could qualify as joy cross her exotic face. Of course, he hadn't known her that long. *Maybe she wears it when she's writing up business contracts.*

Then he remembered the look on her face when they'd been in the locker room at Macalister Enterprises. His body tightened, and he smiled at her. Joy would be fine but he'd definitely like to see passion on her face again. Preferably as soon as possible.

"All right, we're heading into the rapids. Water's a little pushy today so we need to watch out," their trip leader called out. "Everybody remember what we taught you? If you fall out of the boat..."

"Toes to your nose!" the group called out cheerfully. At least, most of them had. Diana seemed to be muttering something under her breath.

"Right! And then one of us will toss you a line or an oar and get you back into the boat. Now let's do this thing!"

And with a whoop, they pushed their raft away from the bank and plunged into the thrashing water.

Finn was yelling and grinning, even though it was a baby ride for him, all things considered. He'd pushed it and signed them up for intermediate rapids because she'd said she liked water, and she had only shrugged when he'd told her his choice. He glanced behind him. She was paddling hard, her teeth bared in a growl. Her eyes gleamed black and glossy, and spray covered her face.

Like a warrior goddess. Pride filled his heart.

Then the boat rocked hard to dodge a boulder. People hollered as if they were on a roller coaster.

"Did you see..." he yelled, then turned.

Diana wasn't there.

"Diana!" he called, and scrambled to look over the side of the raft.

"Man overboard!" one of them yelled, and the two instructors moved instantly.

Finn searched the chop frantically, his heart a ball of lead. "Diana! *Diana!*"

Suddenly, he saw the bob of neon orange and his adrenaline surged.

"Stay in the boat, sir. We've got this," the instructor in the back of the boat snapped, and leaned into the river with his oar extended. Diana gripped it and they tugged her toward the raft, helping her as she struggled to get on board.

"You're okay! You did everything just right," the instructor said.

She looked pale, was all Finn could think. Her eyes looked wild.

"Oh, my God, are you all right? Did you hurt anything?" Finn asked as she settled back into her place. She wrapped her arms around herself—her oar had gone missing.

"I'm fine."

He stared at her. She was now fixated on the water ahead. Other than being chilled, perhaps, she seemed almost bored.

"Holy crap, woman, you are made of *steel,*" he said with admiration. The rest of the boat cheered.

She didn't even crack a smile.

They rode out the rest of the rapids, pulling in at the shore of their campsite. Finn and the others climbed out of the raft immediately. Even for a relatively simple run, the journey had been exhilarating and somewhat exhausting. Diana hadn't said a word the entire time, though she certainly looked tired.

"You starving? I'm starving," he said, throwing an arm around her shoulder. "Congratulations! You survived hazing!"

She shrugged off his arm and headed for the tent.

"What's wrong?" he asked. She should be ecstatic, or at least relieved.

She stopped only long enough to stare at him over her shoulder in complete, disgusted disbelief.

"Okay, what are you pissed at *me* for?" he asked, rushing to catch up with her. But then he realized that she seemed to be limping. "Wait a minute, are you hurt? What happened?"

"Just leave me alone, Finn." Her voice was low and flat. "I don't want to talk to you right now."

He stepped in front of her. "It's only going to fester if you don't talk to me," he said, crossing his arms. "You're upset. You think I did something wrong. Let's talk about this."

She took off her helmet, then drove it right into his stomach. He let out a pained *oof* and grabbed it. Her eyes were murderously dark, her expression one of barely contained rage…and pain.

"I'm not one of your goddamned *Players,* Finn," she hissed. "I didn't sign up for this. I'm here because you and your father seem to have some pissing contest and you both don't seem to care about how *I* feel about participating. So no, Finn, *I don't think I want to talk about this.*"

Shocked, he watched as she limped to her tent, ignoring the startled looks of their fellow rafters. She zipped the flap shut, then let out what sounded like a scream muffled by a pillow. Then she went quiet.

"What the hell's *wrong* with him?" Finn heard a woman rafter mutter to her husband. "If she doesn't like rafting, why did he bring her?"

Finn felt shame lash at him like a whip.

He'd brought her here to prove a point. He'd wanted

to show her that if she just moved out of her comfort zone, she could feel free, happy, joyful.

How's that working out for you, slick?

DIANA WAS ABOUT SIX. She and her mother were...somewhere with a beach. She'd been playing with sand castles, fenced in by the cigarette butts she'd found littered by her mother's friends. A few of them were big men that laughed with a mean sound—she didn't like them.

"Why don't you go in the water?" one of the men said. His laugh sounded like a donkey, and his face was red. He gestured to the lapping waves with his beer bottle. "Come on, honey, you'll have fun."

"Go ahead," her mother insisted.

She shook her head. She didn't want to. She liked her sand castles.

Her mother walked up to her. She had the crazy-eyes today, Diana thought. She grabbed Diana's arm, hard.

"Ow!"

"Go in the damned water," her mother said sharply. "You're not a baby, and I didn't bring you out to the beach so you could do shit you'd do at the sandbox at school!"

So she went in the water. It was cold, colder than she was used to, and she started to step out, onto the rocks. They seemed to stab into the bottom of her feet. She looked at her mother, who was finally smiling. She wasn't going to complain. She wasn't sure what her mother would do if she complained.

The water was moving quick, quicker than she'd guessed. "Mom...?" She ventured a step back toward shore. The rocks were slippery, slick, and she felt an awful sensation as she fell. The water seemed to lift her. But she couldn't find her feet, and she couldn't breathe. Her arms flailed, the water was rushing and dark and her ears pounded and she couldn't breathe, couldn't breathe, couldn't...

DIANA SAT UP WITH A START, gasping, sweating. She rubbed her hand over her face, felt the wet residue of tears.

She was in a tent, she realized slowly. She was camping. Had been white-water rafting. Exhausted, upset, she'd collapsed onto her sleeping bag and fallen asleep.

"Just a nightmare," she told herself. No doubt it had been triggered by falling out of the stupid boat. She hadn't thought of that awful trip her mother had taken her on for a long time. They'd gone to the Sacramento River with a bunch of her junkie friends. She'd hoped it would be such a good time, and it had turned horrible. A nearby fisherman had gone in and rescued her, helping Diana cough out the water. As soon as the fisherman left them, her mother had hit her for going in the water.

Damned if you do, damned if you don't.

Wow. If her life were a movie, she'd probably hit the director for being so frickin' obvious with the theme.

Just get through this.

She sat up, stretching out the kinks. Man, was she hungry. There was supposed to be some sort of barbecue—maybe she'd slept through it?

"Diana?" A tentative whisper.

It was Finn. Of course it was Finn. "What do you want?"

He opened her tent, popping his head inside. "Thought you might want some dinner."

She shrugged, considered denying how hungry she was just to spite him. But not only was that petty, it was an outright and obvious lie. Her stomach started yowling plaintively. "All right, thanks."

She stepped out of the tent, saw that he'd set up a little table for one, complete with lantern and candle. She was reluctantly charmed, but didn't say anything as she sat down in the cloth camp chair. She'd eat quickly, acknowledge his effort, then go back to bed. They'd be on a plane soon enough, anyway…on to her next challenge.

Disneyland, she thought. *What was I thinking?*

"Where is everybody?" she asked instead, scanning the campsite. She'd set her tent up a bit farther away than the others had, as Finn had done…she wasn't really the social type. Still, all the tents were closed up and quiet.

"They're asleep," Finn said, watching her as she bit into her hamburger. It was delicious.

"Really?" she asked, around a bite. "I thought they'd be partying it up all night."

Did she always sound that bitter?

"Nah. The river wipes you out. I've seen this happen dozens of times." He took a deep breath, grabbed a chair and sat down across from her. "Listen, I want to apologize."

She'd just taken a big bite of burger, so she struggled, chewing. "Frr wha?"

He didn't so much as smile. "For earlier. Actually, for hazing you at all," he said. "I thought you said you liked the water."

She managed to swallow. "I do," she clarified, snagging some potato chips. "I like sitting by the ocean, sipping wine, or drinking a cup of coffee at a lakeside cabin. But almost drowning?" She grimaced as the flash-memory of water rushing around her came to mind, the sensation of suffocation hitting her. "Not really my cup of tea."

"God, I'm such a jerk," he muttered.

She stared at him, surprised at the sincerity in his voice. "You were hazing me. The whole point of hazing someone is breaking them down, isn't it? To see if they can handle it…and if they can't, you cut them loose. That makes sense."

"No, it doesn't," he said, looking appalled. "Hazing, for us, means…well, seeing if you can handle getting pushed out of your comfort zone, or if you're going to cry and whine and bitch. It doesn't mean torturing someone or terrifying them, or making them sick."

"It wasn't pleasant, but I'm not sick, and I certainly don't bitch." Although she had, she realized. "Not always, anyway."

"You had every right," Finn said, and for whatever reason, it was a small comfort to her. "So…my dad would've fired you if you didn't come along, huh?"

She blanched. *No, he's going to fire me if I don't tor-*

pedo you. "It's not that big a deal. He's asked me to do worse."

Like what I'll need to do when this month is over.

"You may be the toughest woman I know," Finn said.

She discovered she liked having his respect. "Well, I didn't mean to spout off like that. The water...shook me," she admitted. "And I was resentful because it wasn't my idea. I hate feeling like I'm being set up to fail."

"You should've told me no when we started this," he said. "But you don't tell people you can't or won't do something that often, do you? You think that would make you appear weak. And I think you hate acknowledging you're not good at something."

He might have a point. That fact needled her, and she quickly cleaned off the table.

"At least your other challenges are a walk in the park. Literally," Finn said, with a laugh. "Theme park, anyway. Are you looking forward to it?"

"A full day of kiddie rides. Oh, boy. Hold me back."

"It's not... Never mind. You know, I'll just let you experience it yourself."

"As far as I'm concerned, it's just a job, Finn." She wondered if he was disappointed by her response, and would the same hold true when they were at Disneyland.

Quietly they sat together. The sky wasn't like it was in San Francisco, which seemed to glow orange with the reflection of city lights on cloud cover. It was a deep navy blue, like the kind of blue when light reflects on dark satin. It was littered with brilliant, diamond-twinkling stars. For a second, she felt awed, almost overwhelmed.

"Beautiful, isn't it?"

Finn's voice was right near her ear—she'd been gazing up so intently, she hadn't heard him coming so near her. She could now smell him, his masculine scent deliciously sexy, blending with the woods.

"I don't get a lot of chances to look at the stars," she stammered, knowing that if she turned her head, his face would be right there, next to hers.

And then what would you do?

"Ever made love under the stars?"

Her breasts tightened and her stomach twisted. Now that she knew what his body was capable of, her body sensed the opportunity for a repeat performance. It was lobbying hard for her to go for it.

"I'm still mad at you, Finn," she tried.

"Pretend I'm somebody else, then." She could hear the smile in his voice. "I've always wanted someone to call me Ramon."

It surprised a laugh out of her, which she down-shifted into a sigh. She forced herself out of the chair, and to step away from him. "That thing in the locker room…"

"Oh, yes," he breathed, closing the distance, rubbing her arms lightly with his fingertips.

"It was a mistake, Finn, for both of us. I generally don't sleep with men I don't know, and I certainly don't do it on the premises of Macalister corporate head-quarters."

"Breaking the rules sometimes can be fun, Diana,"

he said, his whispering sending a thrill along her nerve endings. "The unexpected, the forbidden. Didn't you like that?"

She bit her lip. Oh, he knew exactly how much she'd liked that.

He leaned forward, his lips brushing along hers, just enough to tease and taunt, not enough to satisfy.

"I thought you didn't believe in torturing someone," she said, against his mouth.

"Not during hazing, anyway." And he pulled her into his arms.

WHEN SHE RELENTED to kissing him her body went pliant against his, and Finn sent up a silent shout of gratitude. He was finally getting to do what he'd been burning to do since he'd last tasted her. Then, it had been a long shot, a fluke, a deliciously forbidden surprise.

This…well, this time, it was a bit more calculated, admittedly. Even if she said it would never happen again, he'd felt the flash burn of desire between them. He'd felt the way her gaze always seemed to follow him, the way she was unable to stay away even though she was careful not to physically touch him if she could help it. As if she were afraid they'd combust with contact.

And boy, were they ever conbustible.

She was wearing a T-shirt and shorts, and he reached down to cup her ass, pulling her taut against his rock-hard erection. Her grateful moan and the shimmy of her hips rubbing her pelvis against his hardness was enough to have him clutching at her like a drowning man. His tongue traced her lips before plunging between them, coaxing her tongue to play with his. He felt her pointed nipples as she tried to move higher against his chest. She was about five inches shorter than he was.

He solved that by picking her up, encouraging her legs around his waist. It reminded him of the locker room, of plunging into her hot, wet heat, and his knees almost buckled.

She pulled away. "We… I can't… Out here in the open?"

Finn chuckled. He knew that despite Diana's recent escapade, she'd still want privacy if he miraculously managed to convince her to sleep with him. He'd therefore prepared for this contingency. He nipped at her neck as he brought her to his tent.

He'd gotten an inflatable mattress, king-size and fairly bouncy. All right, it was extravagant for a camping trip, but so were the Egyptian cotton sheets and thick pillows. And his tent had a moon roof, and was even now open to the stars. He placed her on the mattress gently. She was panting, her perky breasts heaving enticingly. When she looked up at him, she smiled.

"I've never seen so many stars," she breathed, leaning back against the mattress. Her eyes sparkled like the night sky. "It's so beautiful."

"Beautiful," he murmured, but he wasn't looking at anything but her.

Their gazes locked for what seemed like a long while. Then she reached for her shirt, slipping it off in one motion, revealing a purple bikini top underneath.

As she went for the fly of her shorts, he quickly peeled off his top, his mouth going dry at her look of hungry appreciation. He stripped out of the rest of his clothes as she took off the shorts, then shimmied out of the bikini bottoms and undid the strings to her top. When she was nude, he noticed she had no tan lines: just an even, deliciously creamy almond shade of skin, a stark contrast to the darkness of her hair, her eyes.

He slid down beside her. "I've wanted you," he breathed, nipping at her shoulder, her neck, palming her breasts and kneading gently. She arched her back, filling his hands, reaching for him. He decided to tease her, replacing one of his hands with his mouth. She softly gasped as he suckled her. His hand now free, his fingertips touched the flat planes of her abdomen, then down to the curls between her thighs. Searching gently between the folds, he found the tight, wet passageway. His cock twitched eagerly.

She moaned, parting her legs to give him better access. He twirled his tongue around her nipple as his fingers flicked the tight button of her clit. Her head lolled on the pillow as he worked feverishly. He sucked, then licked and licked again.

He could feel her body pulsing. He shuddered, struggling for his own self-control.

She was breathing hard, her eyes molten bright in the darkness. "Finn," she said, her voice ragged. "Inside me. I want you inside me."

He didn't need to be asked twice. He fished in his bag for a condom, his hands shaking with need. When he returned to her, ready, she rubbed her hands on his chest, rested them on his shoulders as he moved gently between her thighs. Slowly and surely, he pressed forward, until he was buried inside her.

She whispered his name, how good he felt, her nails raking down his back as she rocked her pelvis, urging him deeper. He withdrew, eliciting a protest, then smiled as he pressed forward again, trembling at the feel of her tight passage massaging his shaft.

She wouldn't let him go slow, demanded that he be demanding. Their rhythm sped up. She was moving sinuously, the undulating actions of her body driving him wild. He plunged inside her, moving faster, harder, feeling her thighs squeeze against his hips, and her body shook beneath him.

She orgasmed, again and again. A seemingly endless set of waves crested over him until he thought he'd go crazy with it. His own orgasm hit him and he climaxed in time with her, the sensation overwhelming.

When it finally ended, he twisted so he wouldn't collapse on top of her. Instead, he tugged her on top of him. She stared down at him, a look of sleepy wonder on her face.

"I really like you, Diana."

"I...like you, too."

He wiggled his eyebrows. "Enough to let me do that again? After I, you know, recover?"

She laughed, and it was a great sound.

"If you recover," she said, dipping down to kiss his face, "sure. But I'm still mad at you."

"Let's see if I can't do something about that."

8

STRIDING OUT OF THE Orange County airport, Diana decided she was getting pretty good at this denial stuff. What happened in Colorado would stay in Colorado. And that interlude in the gym at Macalister headquarters? That had to be a stress dream. That never actually *happened* to anyone, outside of late-night porn movies, right?

Absolutely, she convinced herself, as she picked up her light overnight bag and laptop case. It was all a dream. Or it didn't count. Or didn't matter.

That was her story, and she was sticking to it.

Finn was walking next to her, too close, as he brushed against her. "Sorry," he said. The laughter in his eyes was clear.

She bit her lip so she wouldn't smile back. Then the two of them climbed into a limo, winding their way toward Anaheim. It had comfy seats and air-conditioning, so she didn't mind the crawl of L.A. traffic.

Opening her laptop bag, she pulled out her computer and plugged in the adapter. He stared at her setup, amused. "You're going to work? Really?"

She glanced up at him. "Are you kidding? I'm behind as it is." She frowned. "How long do we need to stay at Disneyland for me to fulfill that challenge anyway?"

Finn just shook his head, avoiding her question. Before she could pester him, he started to put up the divider between the driver and the backseat.

"Don't get any wise ideas, funny boy." She scooted farther away from him before her body could hijack her common sense again. "This stupid standard operating manual isn't going to write itself, you know."

He scooted closer to her, his thigh pressing against hers as he glanced at her computer screen. "How's that coming?" he asked, his tone deceptively innocent.

"It's fine," she muttered, elbowing him until he gave her some room. "It's almost halfway done." It really hadn't been as hard as she thought, in some ways. The day to day of her job wasn't that difficult. It was the unexpected weird crap—*like going to Disneyland*—that made her job so much more challenging. No pun intended.

"You're still in your first week, and you've got a full month to finish your challenges...and you've already got your hazing in the bag." He dodged her, hauled away her laptop and closed it. She growled at him. "Diana, part of the point of this is to actually enjoy the challenges, not just cross them off your checklist. It's the journey, not the destination that counts."

"How Zen," she said, sneering. "Do you make this

up as you go along, or is there some voluminous tome of Player's Club codes that I ought to be studying?"

He laughed, and it made her stomach jitter pleasantly. "It's all up here, baby."

"Not all," she murmured, then clenched her teeth shut to prevent any more dumb innuendos from popping out. *Settle down, you,* she chastised. *Wasn't three times last night enough?*

Of course, the blaring answer *NO* was quick and ruthless. She'd better lock it down—they were going to a children's amusement park, for pity's sake.

Finn was grinning, but he was gentlemanly enough not to take advantage of her slip—which she had mixed feelings about. "The Player's Club has a set of guidelines, rather than laws. We have the rules we read in the beginning of the meeting you went to, but that's about it. It's pretty flexible."

So are you, she thought, then closed her eyes. Her libido was apparently trying out for a comedy festival. "How did a guy like you get involved in a thing like this, anyway?"

"What do you mean, a guy like me?" His tone was light, but his expression was irritated. She quickly felt the cold where his warmth had once been. "The lazy, shiftless, useless trust-fund-brat type?"

"I wouldn't have put it exactly like that."

His smile was feral. "Actually, I think you've put it exactly like that."

She'd hurt him, and that was worse than any embarrassment. "I didn't know you," she said quietly. "That's no excuse, though. And now that I know you, I know it isn't true at all."

She gave him an impromptu and apologetic kiss. He looked mollified...and slightly mischievous. Next thing she knew, he'd tugged her onto his lap.

"Hey! No hanky-panky," she said, trying to scramble off him and failing. "Besides, I didn't say you were shiftless, lazy or useless. I don't remember calling you a brat specifically, and you *do* have a trust fund."

"Semantics," he said, nibbling at her earlobe. She let out a sigh before she could catch herself.

"You spend an awful lot of time with the Player's Club," she said, her eyes crossing as he worked more intently. "It's like you run the place."

"I started it," he replied, surprising her through the sensual haze he was creating. "Well, Linc and I did, anyway. Nine years ago."

Shocked, she pulled back enough to search his face. "Really?"

He looked as if she'd goosed him. "What?"

"You started the Player's Club?" she asked. "That's amazing! Why? How?"

He stared at her, obviously baffled. "I totally did not mean to tell you that," he marveled, then smirked. "You've been seducing secrets out of me, lady."

"But..." Before she could ask any more questions, he was kissing her, hard, and pressing her against the cushions of the limo. Her body responded instantly, wanting more.

You are not going to be so cliché as to have sex in

a limo, she scolded herself...then gasped. *Maybe one quick...*

There was a knocking on the partition. "We're here, sir."

She shoved Finn off her, desperate to straighten her clothes. "What *is* it with you?"

"You started it," he said, winking at her, and her jaw dropped.

"I did not!"

Finn opened the door, and she followed, still protesting...until she saw that they weren't at the park. "We're checking into the resort?"

He nodded. "You can't do a few hours at Disneyland, honey. I got four day passes to both parks. You'll have a blast."

She was going to protest when she turned and saw a mountain. And a big tower. And a...good grief, that was a roller coaster in the shape of Mickey Mouse's head.

"Oh, okay," she huffed, suddenly feeling unsure. It looked...well, sort of cool. Probably ridiculous, but it also looked intriguing. "It's your Club. I'll follow the rules."

"Big of you." He grabbed her bags and they checked in to the hotel. Then they took the monorail. She felt an unfamiliar feeling, a sort of tingling rush that she'd only equated with Finn. As they entered the park, her eyes went wide.

"It's like...some old-fashioned little town," she remarked, awestruck. There were teeming crowds of people, and lots of kids, but lots of adults, too. There was a barbershop quartet singing in striped jackets and flat-brimmed straw hats. There were horse-drawn trolleys. She glimpsed a map posted nearby.

"This is *all* here?" she said, suddenly overwhelmed. And it had been here all this time, without her knowing about it?

Another flash memory. *Don't worry, baby, someday I'll take you to Disneyland. Now let Mommy sleep, okay?*

Diana closed her eyes, fighting unexpected tears.

Finn noticed. She knew he noticed. She could only be grateful when he didn't comment on them. Instead, he surprised her, taking her by the hand.

"What do you want to see first?"

All of it, she thought, but squeezed his hand.

"Surprise me," she said, smiling. It shouldn't be a problem: he surprised her all the time.

IT WAS AROUND MIDNIGHT when Finn and Diana returned to the hotel. He'd requested a suite. Diana had all but skipped into her room, saying something about being "too wired to sleep," and he wasn't sure if that was code for "I want to make mad, crazy love to you" or what, but he sort of hoped he could get in a catnap before that happened.

How far the mighty have fallen. Lincoln would be laughing his ass off if he could see Finn right now.

But hell, Finn thought as he kicked off his shoes and collapsed on his bed. They'd done practically everything in the park. Diana had been like a six-year-old. She'd screamed her way through Space Mountain and Star Tours and the Matterhorn. She'd watched the kids playing at the giant water fountains; she'd dragged him through Sleeping Beauty's tower and even on the carousel. He'd bought her a hat with ears, and a princess T-shirt. She was glowing, almost speechless with happiness.

He smiled to himself. It might not have been an adrenaline-pumping thrill ride, but he felt happier, and strangely more alive, than he had in a very long time. He'd been enchanted, and it had nothing to do with the fairy-tale kingdom.

Before he could think about that for too long, his phone rang. He expected it to be Lincoln. "Yeah?" he grunted.

"Dude, it's Ben!" The kid sounded excited, as he always did. "What happened to you, man? Been trying to reach you for two days! You fell off the face of the earth?"

"Stuff came up," replied Finn, rolling his eyes, but then immediately feeling guilty. "How's the cannonball stuff coming?"

"Oh, that's covered. Next week, Vegas." Ben sounded bored. "That'll be a snap. I was really pretty bummed that they don't actually, you know..."

"Shoot you out of a cannon," Finn said. "Yeah, I can see how that'd be a letdown."

"But Everest is going to be *epic,*" Ben said enthusiastically. "I've got the sherpas, the travel stuff, the equipment. Everything's going according to plan. Just a few more weeks, and we'll be *there,* man!"

"Everest. Epic," he repeated, wondering why he

wasn't feeling more enthusiastic about the trip. Why he wasn't feeling much of anything.

He was used to feeling pretty numb most of the time. But when even Everest couldn't get his blood pumping…come on, what was left?

"So anyway, I thought you could come by tomorrow, look over the stuff. Just to make sure I'm on the right track. And do you think we could get any of the other Players to go?"

"Um, Ben, I'm out of town," Finn interrupted, before Ben could plow forward. "But as soon as I get back in San Francisco, we'll take care of it."

"Oh." Ben sounded disappointed, and Finn grimaced.

"I'm sorry. This… I've got some personal family stuff that's come up. And, er…" He glanced at the bedroom door, hearing Diana humming "It's a Small World," charmingly off-key. "Woman stuff, actually."

"Really?" Ben sounded surprised, then asked, "Is she hot?"

"Hell, yeah," Finn blurted, before shaking his head. "It's a long story. When were you doing Vegas and the cannon?"

"Next week."

Finn thought of Diana's challenges. "Maybe we can swing by," he mused, speculating about what Diana's impression of Vegas would be. Then he grinned. "Okay. Text me the details. I'll get in touch with you soon."

"Great. But I want to nail this Everest plan down soonest," Ben said, impatiently. "Man. I'd go *tomorrow* if I could!"

Finn said goodbye and hung up. He looked at his phone, pensive.

Diana was at the doorway. “You okay?”

“Yeah,” he said, shutting the phone off. “Just feeling a little…old.”

She stared at him, then laughed. “How old are you?”

“Twenty-nine.”

“Oh, yeah. You’re ancient.” She twirled next to the bed. “I, on the other hand, am thirty-five. And I feel about…three, I think.”

He smiled at her. “And you look really happy.” He felt some of the numbness recede.

“I don’t think I can sleep,” she said, bouncing on her toes. “I never would have thought…never would have *guessed*… I’m sorry. I’m incoherent. I feel drunk or something.” She laughed gloriously. “Hyper!”

“Well,” he drawled, reaching for her. “The park doesn’t open till morning, sweetie. What are we going to do with all that energy?”

She smiled wickedly. Then she reached down. She was wearing a pink T-shirt. When she peeled it off, she was a wearing a petal-pink lace bra, with a matching thong and garter belt, complete with a white satin rose in the front.

“Hmm.” He leaned back as she started to straddle him and work on his fly. “If it’ll help you sleep…”

9

Two days after the great Disneyland adventure, Diana was back into her normal routine. She was at her desk, but felt slightly disoriented. It had been longer than she could remember since she'd taken a full week and a half off work, and she'd never gone white-water rafting and spent four days at an amusement park. Technically, it was work, but it wasn't like any work she was aware of. It had been pure fun. She'd opted to go back into the office and hopefully finish off her manual while Finn went to Vegas to…well, get shot out of a cannon, she thought, foolishly grinning.

Seriously. Who else could she say that about? *I'm going to have to reschedule—I'm getting shot out of a cannon on Wednesday.* It was ludicrous. Wild. Amazing.

It was vintage Finn.

Where it once used to strike her as annoying, it had somehow switched and become endearing.

Perhaps all the sex had some influence on that.

"Morning, Penny," she called out to her assistant. Diana hoped she wasn't blushing.

Her assistant stared at her, slack-jawed. "Um, morning," she replied finally, stepping into her office. "Guess *you* had a good time."

"Hmm?" Diana sighed, feeling some of her Disneyland-Finn high dissipate as she noted the spreadsheet open on her laptop. She sensed her shoulders beginning to tighten.

"You look…" Penny paused meaningfully. *"Relaxed."*

"I got some rest," she agreed, although now that she thought about it, she hadn't really. Between the park all day and Finn most of the night, she'd averaged about twelve hours of sleep over four days. Yet, for whatever reason, she'd been energized.

Now, after eight straight hours of slumber, why did she feel exhausted?

She frowned. The job was stressful, yes. But she also loved it. She *loved* solving problems. She loved finding solutions to things that people thought were impossible. Even the technical, eye-crossing details of contracts were like a puzzle for her. And while Thorn was a pain in the ass, he genuinely valued her.

So why was she suddenly so tense?

"Big boss wants an…update," Penny said, still staring at Diana.

"Okay, *what's wrong?*" Diana asked finally, standing up. "You're freaking me out."

"You just look so…" Penny struggled for a description. *"Loose."*

Diana blinked. And blushed.

"Oh, no, I didn't mean..." Penny said, then her eyes narrowed, and she glanced out the door to see if anyone would overhear. "Did you get lucky?" she asked, in a quiet, incredulous tone.

"Penny," Diana said, mortified. "Really? Do we need to talk about this?"

"You've gone from being tight as a size two to mellow as a Berkeley hippie," Penny said wryly. "If you're going to tell me you just got this relaxed from taking a vacation, I'm going to book the next flight to Colorado with connections in Anaheim."

"Actually," Diana said, smiling gently, "I went to Disneyland."

Penny's eyes almost popped out of her head. "Seriously? Like, the park?"

Diana nodded.

"I wouldn't have pegged you for a Disney fan," Penny said. "But, you know, good for you."

"Um, thanks?"

"Sorry, that sounded weird." Penny crossed her arms over her chest. "But you've been so stressed lately, especially with whatever the Finn business was. It's nice to see you so calm."

Penny left, and Diana knew the smile on her own lips had faltered.

The Finn business.

Her phone rang, and she picked it up. "Diana Song," she answered, forcing herself to shift into business mode.

"What are you wearing?"

She burst into laughter, causing Penny to return, clearly curious. Diana motioned to Penny to close the door. "Black business suit, peach blouse, sensible heels."

"Yeah, but what are you wearing under *that?*"

She felt her cheeks heat, even as she chuckled some more. "What if I said nothing?"

"Uh-huh, am now picturing that." He paused. "If this keeps up, I'm not going to be able to fit in the cannon's barrel, sticking out like this."

"Vivid," she murmured.

"I miss you."

She stammered, stunned. "I…"

"I know, we barely know each other. But you're fun."

She blinked. Intelligent, ambitious, even sexy. But *fun?*

When had anyone ever called her that?

"You're fun, too," she said.

"And sexy as hell," he prompted.

"Well, yes…" she drawled.

"Ever had phone sex?"

She snorted, then lowered her voice to a hiss. "I am *not* doing that in my office." Even as part of her was admittedly intrigued.

"You haven't, have you?" From the sound of his voice, she'd bet anything he had a wicked gleam in his eye. "God, I love a challenge."

"You…"

There was a curt knock at her door, and Thorn strode in without waiting. "We need to talk," he told her.

"Thorn," she said, standing up and almost strangling herself with the phone cord. "Um…"

"Damn it," Finn said. "That sure ruins the mood. I'll call you later, sexy."

"Right. Later." She hung up the phone with a clatter.

"So how did it go?" Thorn stared at her, expectant, and crossed his arms.

She forced herself to clear her head, damning Finn and his phone calls, and the way her body seemed to heat when he said something as simple as *Hi.*

"I finished the hazing and the first challenge," she said. "I only have to finish the manual and, ah, take that vacation to Paris, and I'll be in."

"Paris? Really?" Thorn looked irritated. "Did you just cook this up with my son so you could get some paid vacation time, or what?"

Automatically, her chin rose. "I could keep it local. We could always skydive, blindfolded and naked. Doing shots of absinthe." She paused. "While shooting skeet."

Thorn tried to stare her down, but she was too angry.

"Knowing my son, that's probably a possibility," he conceded. "So you're saying I should be grateful that you're keeping the challenges safe, if still extravagant?"

She wasn't actually saying that, but if it worked for him, so be it. She simply crossed her arms to match his pose.

He ran a hand through his silver hair, a gesture of frustration that reminded her of Finn. "I swear to God, I will sleep easier when this month is over," he said, leaning against her glass desktop. "Does he suspect?"

"Suspect what?"

Thorn growled. "Suspect that you're going to torpedo him."

Diana felt her breath catch for a moment. "No," she said, and her stomach roiled. "No, he doesn't suspect."

"Good." Thorn let out a deep breath. "It's going to be hard for him to take, but it's the best way, I think. If he knew that you were going to drop the hammer on him, so to speak, he'd probably pull out the stops to convince you to change your mind. He's damned persuasive, and he's like a Sherman tank when he decides he wants something."

"Can't imagine where he got that from," Diana demurred, even as her heart rate pounded.

Thorn's laugh was tired. "I'll admit, I'm glad he has a strong personality. And if he'd just stop trying to get killed all the time, I'd probably be okay with whatever he decided to do. But this death wish crap has got to stop. It's killing Betty, and frankly, it's rough on me."

Diana felt sympathy for her boss. He cared, a lot, even if he seemed like a total egomaniac. Still…

"If you'd really be okay with him giving up the Club and the death wish stuff and doing his own thing," she ventured, "you could've had that. You didn't need to agree to this crazy scheme."

He stared at her, frowning.

"So why am I going to Paris, Thorn?"

"You know," he said, "you and Betty are probably the only people who call me on this sort of thing."

She held her breath.

"I'll admit it. I want him to follow in the family business," Thorn said. "He would be great at it. And I want the company to go to somebody in the family. I want another Macalister on the board. I want that very badly."

"So you're pulling a Sherman tank move."

He nodded. "I wouldn't be able to, if I didn't trust you so much," he said, putting a hand on her shoulder and looking fiercely into her eyes. "I know that you're going to back me up. If I didn't, I wouldn't let you handle this situation at all."

She swallowed hard. "You've always believed in me. That does mean a lot."

"I saw it when you interned here as a law student. You're hungry, you're smart and you're unstoppable." He sounded matter-of-fact, and it touched her more than a list of fluffy accolades. "So don't disappoint me, Diana. I want Finn working here. Don't let him change your mind."

With that, he turned to leave. "Enjoy Paris. We've got a ton of things coming up and I think it's going to be a long damned time before you're able to vacation again."

He went, and she felt adrift.

"Hey, could you sign..." Penny said, entering Diana's office. She stopped, giving Diana a long look. "Well, that didn't take long."

"What didn't?" She was starting to get a headache.

Penny sighed, pulling a bottle of ibuprofen out of her pocket and reaching in the minifridge for a cold bottle of water. "For the tension to return. You went from light as a feather to a block of concrete in about five minutes." She handed the water and the pills to Diana.

"Great." Diana popped three of the pills into her mouth with a glug from the bottle.

"Maybe you can do…more of whatever you did before," Penny suggested.

Diana sighed, thinking of Finn. The sexy, adventurous, caring, funny guy who thought she was amazing.

It figured. To back the one man who'd ever trusted her, she was going to have to betray the only one she'd ever fallen in love with.

IT WAS SIX-THIRTY and George was at the bar. He'd done the stultifying, stupid busywork that he had to, and attended several mind-numbing meetings that seemed both repetitive and interminable. Not to mention his going in on time—largely—and leaving late. Well, late enough, especially for a Macalister.

Oh, yeah, he'd *earned* this drink, and gulped down two manful swigs of his martini.

Alex, the bartender, already had his second martini ready. George smiled thinly, reaching for the second drink before his first was finished. "Thanks, man. Work was a bitch."

Alex didn't respond, which was just as well. George didn't feel like pouring out his problems to the help, anyway, he thought with a sniff.

"There's our hardworking man," Jonesy said, claiming the bar stool next to him. "But chin up, my man, it's all in a good cause. Alex? Set me up with the usual."

Alex nodded silently, and had the neat whiskey in front of Jonesy before he'd finished his sentence…and had the second one set up, as well. Jonesy smiled expansively.

Jonesy might have a problem, George thought, toying with his olive.

Jonesy took a sip of his whiskey, then said, "Come on. Let's move this to a booth, shall we? I don't feel like screaming every word."

Something private, then, George thought with a frown, grabbing both martini glasses. They trekked to the far side of the bar, ignoring and ignored by the business-suited happy hour folks. George waited until Jonesy sat down, then said quietly, "What's going on? Everything all right?" Not that he cared, so much, but there was something about Jonesy that was ever so slightly unstable. If there was a problem, it might be better to know before things got out of hand.

"Oh, not to worry," Jonesy said, draining his first glass and putting it down with a soft thump on the table. He glanced around. "Your boy Victor lacks spine, that's all."

George sighed. He'd been losing a bit of his spine, too, knowing that Diana was going to be on the case when the month was over. Why he'd believed Victor had the skills to pull this off, he'd never know. "Uncle Thorn's made it clear, he wants another Macalister on the board, and he wants to groom an heir. Finn's a fuckup. That leaves me."

Jonesy shrugged. "Seems to me that leaves a lot to chance. What if Finn straightens up?"

"He won't," George said darkly. "He wouldn't leave the Club."

"I had Victor do some more digging," Jonesy said casually, even though there was an edge to his normally genial voice. "Seems like there's a bet in the works. That cousin of yours bet your uncle that he could prove the Club was a worthwhile venture, or some such."

"I know, remember?" George glowered. "Son of a bitch." He drank some more of his martini.

"Well, did you know this?"

Jonesy spread a few photos on the table. They were of Diana and Finn, at Disneyland, from the looks of it. Diana was laughing. In one photo, Finn was feeding her ice cream, they were laughing at a restaurant.

In the third photo, more grainy and night-vision green, they were definitely doing more than laughing.

George felt fury pushing at the back of his eyes until he thought his head would explode. *"Son of a bitch!"*

"You said that," Jonesy said calmly. "Obviously your cousin is pulling out all the stops to get this bird on his side, yeah?"

George took a few deep breaths. Then he drained the rest of his drink and motioned to the waitress. "I knew he was sneaky, but I didn't know he'd sink this low."

"Like you wouldn't do the same," Jonesy clucked. "But it's something we now need to deal with. I'm starting to think that things are swinging in your cousin's favor. When she gets back, she's going to tell your uncle that the Player's Club is like the Boy Scouts, she's going to smile and play nice, and she's probably going to keep screwing the heir apparent."

Bile filled George's throat. "Damn it. *Damn it.*"

Jonesy tucked the photos back into a briefcase.

"Great that you're angry, Georgie, but right now you have to *think*." He snapped his fingers in front of George's face, and George growled at him. "She's going to also come back and step right into this financial situation of ours. If it starts to point toward you..."

George felt the blood drain from his face. "Finn will tell her to come after me," George said, shaking. "He hates me. She'll nail me to the wall."

Jonesy nodded like some kind of guru. "I suspected as much. So, what are our options here?"

"I don't know."

The waitress put a martini down on their table. George grabbed at it, waving her away.

Jonesy took it from him.

"What the hell?" George snarled.

"Before you drown your sorrows and become completely useless to me," Jonesy said, with venom in his voice, "I told you—we need a plan."

"Victor was right! We need to put the money back. We'll have to come up with something else," George said, his palms sweaty. "We've *got* to."

"My portion's spoken for, mate," Jonesy said, "and you promised me another quarter mil."

"A quarter mil? Jonesy, how are we supposed to get *that?*" George goggled. "You need to give your portion back!"

Jonesy's laugh was cold enough to sober George up. He knew what his gut had been trying to tell him all along: Jonesy was scary. Scarier than George had wanted to admit.

"I'm not giving it back as it's already spent," Jonesy

commented, matter-of-factly. "And I'm not getting out of this without the money we agreed on, so get that out of your head. First, we make sure this bitch doesn't screw up our plans. I've got Victor working on a way to see this happens.... It's a bit sloppy, but I think it'll hold up. And if that doesn't work, well, there are other methods to take care of our snoopy little lawyer."

George coughed loudly. "Are we sure Victor will play ball?"

"Oh, we won't have any more feet dragging from Victor," Jonesy said, a small, knowing smile on his lips.

George glanced at his watch. "He wasn't at the office this morning—I didn't see his car. I thought he'd be here tonight."

"He's indisposed." At George's puzzled expression, Jonesy's smile broadened. "Don't worry, George, it's just a broken leg. He can still work a computer. That's why I didn't break his arms."

The words sank into George's psyche like blocks of cement into a lake.

Jonesy passed the martini over, and George took it silently.

"I'm in charge now, George," Jonesy announced, sounding as jovial as Santa. "It's all well in hand. I'll take care of this...one way or another."

10

"I CAN'T BELIEVE YOU'VE never been to Paris," Finn marveled.

They were sitting at a small table at the legendary Les Deux Magots café, sipping rich coffee and eating a terrific sort of pastry that Finn couldn't even pronounce. Diana was wearing a silky sundress and some kind of stylish-but-comfy shoes. Her smile was serene. "The place agrees with you. Seriously—if you were wearing a beret, I'd think you were a native."

She gave him a seriously cute wink, tucking her chin down and coyly looking at him through her long lashes. "I've been to Paris before."

"You have?" He frowned. "But I thought—"

"I was here on the way to a conference in...Prague, I think." She took another long sip of coffee. "I remember changing planes at De Gaulle, and wondering what it was like in the city."

Finn grinned. "And?"

"Everything I hoped it would be," she confessed, finishing the last bite of her fruit tart thing. "Better than I imagined."

"Better than Disneyland?"

"Different," she amended. Soon she seemed worried again.

He found himself reaching over, holding her hand. "You seem sadder here. What's up?"

She tugged her hand away, brushing crumbs off her lap. "Why don't we take a walk?" She was pushing it, sounding abnormally cheerful, and he knew something was wrong.

"Come on," he said, pulled her alongside him. "What'd I do?"

"You didn't do anything," she said, with a small, wistful grin. "I just… What are we doing, Finn?"

"We're having a good time. At least, I was." He paused. "Diana, I know what my reputation's like…."

"That's not the problem!" she protested. "I certainly wouldn't judge."

His eyebrows jumped up. "You wouldn't?"

She blushed. "I mean, I don't have comparative experience to yours, but I…I don't care one way or the other."

They wandered down the picturesque boulevard, negotiating the streets toward the Seine River. They continued along the beautiful left bank; Notre Dame loomed in the distance. Diana stopped talking, stopped walking and simply stared for a long minute.

"It's so beautiful," she breathed.

He'd seen this view a million times: family vacations, college trips, parties. Now, with her, it was as if he'd never seen it before. He'd certainly never paid attention before.

He stroked her hair. She made things new. She made things alive.

"I don't want this to just be casual," he said quietly. "It isn't casual. I know, these are weird circumstances, but I would really like to see where this goes, Diana."

He balked when he saw tears starting to well in her eyes.

"What's wrong?" he repeated, rubbing at her cheeks gently with his thumbs.

"Finn…we don't make sense." Her voice broke. "You're my boss's son. You're younger than me. We're from two totally different worlds."

"Does any of that really matter?" He was more amused than concerned.

Temper lit her teary eyes. "I'm only here because your father ordered me here. It's been wonderful, and I see now why this Club means so much to you. But at the end of the day, *I work for your father.*"

"So what? Why does that matter?" he repeated.

She stared at him for a long silent moment. His anger slowly inched up; his vulnerability increased.

"Do you really think when we get back, I'm going to tell your dad that he's losing his little bet?"

"What?"

She let out a huff of breath. "Did you know he gave the okay for my scholarship to law school? He said he saw potential in me," she said, with a note of pleading. "He trusted me with one of the most important jobs in his company, when I was only thirty. I've been in that job for five years. Do you think that he would've sent me here if there were any, absolutely *any* chance that I'd betray him?"

The truth of her words hit him. "You…you would sleep with me, pretend to be having a great time…and then stab me in the back?"

"I am not pretending. I'm having a wonderful time. The best time I've ever had in my life," she whispered passionately, holding him, the expression on her face one of deep pain. "But I report to your father. I'd lose my job, my reputation. I'd lose everything that means anything to me."

He took a careful step away from her. He'd never been so numb. "I'm feeling so stupid here," he said. "I was under the impression that I was starting to mean something to you."

She reached for him, and he took another step.

"Or was I just part of the job?"

Now she was the one who stepped back, as if slapped. "No. Finn, you can't possibly believe that."

"I don't know. I mean, I was stupid enough to trust my father, right?" His laughter was bitter.

"I didn't mean for things to go this far." She was crying now, tears streaming down that toasted almond skin of hers. "I…I do care for you, Finn."

"Please. Let's not do this," he said. "We're becoming a mix of Fellini and a bad Lifetime movie. Let me just cut my losses with some dignity, okay?"

He started to walk away, and she grabbed him, nailed him with a hard, fierce kiss. "I'm so sorry," she said, leaning her forehead against his chest.

"I'm sort of glad," he said. "I mean, normally it takes years for somebody to figure out they're not as important to someone as a job. We nailed it in about two and a half weeks."

He pried her loose, his heart tearing with every motion. When he'd finally disentangled her, he forced his voice to stay level.

"I can ask the hotel to get you another room, if the suite's not big enough."

"Finn..." She was sobbing now.

"Otherwise, I'll wander around for a bit, I think. I've been here tons, don't worry." *As if she would.* He'd been jaded about women before, but this was ridiculous. "I'll see you before we get back to San Francisco. And under the circumstances, I guess you can forgo the whole operating manual thing. That was a lame challenge anyway."

"I'll keep my word."

He raised one eyebrow. "Why start now?"

With that, he walked away blindly, away from Diana and everything that seemed beautiful about Paris.

DIANA WAS SITTING in the sumptuous living room of their hotel suite when Finn came in, sometime after four o'clock in the morning. She'd been out of her mind with worry, and with guilt. She wanted to rush to his side, if only to reassure herself that he was all right.

One look at him proved that he was anything but.

"What happened?" she asked, before the smell of alcohol almost knocked her off her feet.

"I did what seemed appropriate." He was overenunciating, trying to be clear through the pronounced slur. "It's funny…I can speak French when I'm drunk. Want to hear? Bluh bluh bluh, bonjour."

"Yeah, you're multilingual," she said, torn between irritation and concern. She'd never seen him this wretchedly bent. "How much did you have there, Pierre?"

He laughed hoarsely. "Pierre. Good one. Dunno. Stopped counting."

He staggered toward his room, and promptly crashed into a spindly legged end table. "Come on," she said, hoisting his arm over her shoulder. "I'll help you get to bed."

"Haven't gotten enough, huh?" he huffed, as he stumbled along, cracking his knee sharply on the door frame. He howled in pain.

"Well, watch where you're going!" she snapped. Thankfully, the European rooms were small compared to, say, a suite in Vegas. She let him fall like an axed tree onto the bed. "Good night!"

She started to retreat, then noticed…he still had his shoes on, his knees were hanging off the bed. He'd be horribly uncomfortable. She couldn't just leave him like this.

She grabbed his feet to yank off his sneakers, but his shoes were laced too tight. "Of course."

"Diana…"

"They'll be off in a second."

"No," he muttered. "Gonna be…"

And promptly was sick over the side of the bed.

"Oh, *lovely.*" She winced.

By six in the morning, she was starting to freak out. He was violently ill, even though he had nothing left in his stomach and he was ghost pale, sweating bullets.

"I think you might need to go to the hospital, Finn," she said, wiping his face with a cool cloth, helping him lean over to reach the wastebasket one more time. "I think you're really, really sick."

"No," he croaked. "No…no hospitals. I've spent enough time in hospitals."

His eyes were closed, and he looked like he was in a lot of pain—but he was too twisted around to sleep, despite his obvious exhaustion.

"I guess that shouldn't surprise me," she said, just to say something.

"What shouldn't surprise you?"

"All the hospital visits." She smiled gently, brushing the sweat-soaked bangs from his forehead. "Considering you've been in the Player's Club for nine years, I'll bet there are E.R. doctors that know you by your first name."

Finn didn't even smile. "When I was a kid. Lots of damned hospitals. Swore I'd never eat frickin' Jell-O again."

"When you were a kid?" He was the drunk one, the sick one. So why was she having so much trouble following this conversation?

"Cancer."

Her heart stopped for a second. "You had cancer?"

"In remission," he said. He never opened his eyes. "That's why I hate hospitals. Spent enough time in them. Hell, spent enough time in my house, kept in a practical bubble…just so my parents wouldn't see me back in one." He shook his head. "Like keeping me a prisoner would stop it. Like *anything* would."

"Could…could it come back now?" The thought of him, so vibrant, so amazing… Her stomach tightened like a fist.

What if I lost him?

"Always can." His voice was matter-of-fact.

"And you're okay with that?" How could he sound so…so casual?

He cracked open an eye, staring at her. "What do you think?"

Then, suddenly, like a puzzle all the pieces fell together.

The stunts. The adrenaline addiction.

"That's why you started it," she murmured. "The Player's Club."

Finn turned over onto his side, shivering. She covered him with a blanket. "Lincoln and I. He was in for cracking up his car—I was in for my last bout of chemo, from my last round with the big C. And we got to talking and…we just talked about what we hadn't done, wished we'd done. It sort of became a thing."

Her admiration of him grew in one big pulse. "And then…?"

"Went skydiving."

"Had you always wanted to?"

"God, no," he groaned, and it surprised a laugh out of her. "You think you're seeing puking here…I was so scared, I almost peed myself. I cursed at Lincoln the entire way down."

"Then what?"

"Then I felt more alive than I ever have in my life." Despite the sickness, his weak voice sounded proud, happy. "It was the ultimate rush. We kept doing stuff, knocking out our list. Then we tried adding new stuff. Then, on a fluke, I asked George if he wanted to join."

"George?" she blinked. "The weasel?"

"He wasn't always a weasel," Finn said, then laughed. "Okay, he was always a weasel. But when I was a kid, when I was sick, he was always doing stuff. Sneaking me candy, things like that."

"If you've got cancer, you shouldn't have candy!" she said. "It makes it worse, doesn't it?"

"What can I say? He thought he was doing the right thing, and I thought he was pretty cool for a while there. He used to take me drinking and stuff in college. Anyway, I brought him on board, then Lincoln brought on a friend, and it sort of…grew. And it made it all fun. Seeing people change like that."

"An even bigger rush."

His eyes were closing, his exhaustion finally taking over. "Something like that."

She washed his face. "You're a good man, Finn Macalister."

"Don't let it get out," he said, snuggling into his pillow. "Got a rep to uphold."

He fell asleep, and she stared at him for long minutes.

He was a good man, she thought. And now that she knew, she couldn't blame him for how he behaved. If she knew she might die any day, would she have the guts to do half the stuff he'd done?

Would you quit your job?

She stared out the window. Her job was the only thing that had showed she meant anything in the world. It was the only thing she valued.

Until now, she thought, and smoothed the blanket over Finn's sleeping body.

11

Finn decided to book the private plane to hurry them back to the Bay Area. He'd originally had romantic intentions. Now, between Diana's revelation that she was about to completely betray him—on his father's orders—and the mortifying aftermath of his drunken episode and his decision to tell her all about his past and his cancer...

Well, it was enough to make him not want to be in the same country as Diana, much less the same air space.

She kept sending him these soulful looks, which only made the situation worse. "Isn't there a movie you want to watch?" he said sharply. "Or...I don't know, *work* that you want to do?"

"I guess I deserve that," she said. "If it's any comfort, I'm glad you opened up to me."

"It isn't, and I'm not," he retorted. Yes, it might be childish, but he sank into his own seat, opening up his iPad. He scrolled through movies until the battery died and realized he hadn't brought an outlet converter, so he couldn't charge the damned device.

Now he was stuck. He should've bought a book at the damned airport.

"Did you want to use my laptop?" she asked, her tone subdued. "I'm done with my manual, so I won't need to use it for the rest of the flight."

"Your manual?" He scoffed. "Why did you even bother? You didn't want anything to do with the Player's Club anyway. What's the point?"

"I'd started," she said, stretching out on the large gray leather seats. "So I figured I might as well finish."

"That's you. Dedicated. If your job says do it, you do it."

Her chin rose as if on cue. At least it was preferable to this kicked-puppy martyr expression she'd been sporting for the past twelve hours. And how the hell did she occupy the moral high ground to pull *that* look off? he wondered.

"My job is important to me," she said quietly. "It's my life. I don't suppose you'd understand."

"Why? Because I've never had a job in my life?" He didn't mean to bark the words, but his temper got the better of him. He was still too hot to handle at this point. "Because I'm a useless freak who's coasting on his inheritance? Listen up, sweetheart, a lot of my money comes from a lawsuit. I almost died when they used the wrong chemo on me. My parents went for blood. I netted a few mil, and they kept it in a bank account for me. So yeah, I don't work for it, but I guess from a certain point of view you could say I earned it."

"Who are you trying to convince here, Finn? Because the only one who bitches about you being a useless trust fund kid is *you.*"

He tried to look away, look anywhere…but as plush and luxurious as the plane was, it was still a private jet, not Air Force One. He had nowhere to go, no way to escape her relentless reasoning.

She got up and sat down across from him. "If you'd do me the courtesy of listening, like I listened to you, I would feel better."

Now he felt small. He grumped, then nodded.

She seemed…numb. He knew that look. He'd seen that look in the mirror often enough.

"I've told you how I got the job at Macalister. I told you that your father approved my law school scholarship—*indebted* doesn't even cover it."

He sighed. "Yeah, I can imagine."

"No, you really can't." Her voice remained a soft monotone. There was something in its intensity that finally made him shut up and listen to her. "I grew up in Oakland. Broke. My mom was a junkie. I don't even know who my father was. When I was born, she pretty much just smoked pot and partied. My Chinese grandmother was the one who raised me."

Reeling from the revelation, Finn grasped at the only hope he could sense in her small story. "Your grandmother must've been a good influence."

"Not really. She was the one growing the weed."

Finn started to respond, then knew he had nothing to say that could make what she was saying any less painful. He closed his mouth.

"I grew up in a family of criminals, Finn. Not a huge, organized mafia sort of thing. But they were thieves nonetheless that sold stolen goods. Hustlers, dealers, scammers, con artists. Despite that, they were fanatically loyal to one another. That's why I was never taken and put into foster homes. When my mom's addiction progressed—" only the slightest bobble revealed the pain behind her softly spoken words "—I was shuttled off to one aunt or another. I don't even know what I would've become if it weren't for libraries."

"You decided you didn't want anything to do with any of it." He said that firmly.

"I had a cousin who made it out. He went straight, became a lawyer. He was the only one I knew that wasn't sleazy. He worked for the district attorney." Her grin was wide; obviously the memory was a good one. "He had to move out of state, my family was so pissed at him. But he really inspired me. I thought, hey, I could do that. I could be a lawyer. I was already taking care of my mom and dealing with a lot of the English paperwork for the rest of my family, helping them dodge things."

Finn stared at her, fascinated. "So you went to college."

"On scholarship. Then law school. They almost wouldn't let me in, didn't have the money...until I interviewed for a special grant from Macalister Enterprises. I met your dad for all of two minutes. He looked at me, nodded, and said, 'You look like you'd kick some ass.' Next thing I heard I'd got the money."

"That sounds like my dad, actually," Finn said,

with reluctant fondness. His father had a way of sizing people up quickly. And he was often right.

"It felt like a miracle. And later, when he offered the internship at Macalister, I couldn't say no. I didn't want to. I wanted to prove that I was worth it and sort of… pay off my debt."

"Then you were hired and promoted."

"He trusted me," she said. "I'd never had anybody trust me like that."

They were quiet for a long while.

"Do you see your family anymore?" Finn asked, stroking her hand. He couldn't even remember when he'd reached for it.

"No. Not for years." She took a deep breath. "My job's my life, Finn. I can't help what I feel for you, but I also can't help what this means to me. I can't throw it all away, just like that. Not for something so new. And I wish you could understand, although I know why you won't. I'm destroying the thing that means the most to you. Of course you'll hate me."

"I don't hate you," he said, tugging at her until she was sitting at his side. He put an arm around her shoulders. "I'm mad. I'll admit that. But there's a way around it. There's a solution we're not seeing."

He kissed her cheek, tasting the salt of the tears that were starting to pour down her cheeks. "Hell, you're the Hammer, aren't you? Don't you pull off incredible crap all the time?"

"With everything but my personal life," she said, with a hiccupy laugh. "Jeez. I've cried more this month with you than I have in the past ten years."

"I have that effect on women," he joked. "Listen, why don't we do something about that?"

She blinked. "You can't possibly mean..."

His body started to heat. "Try me."

SHE SMILED. PART OF HER, the rational part of her, knew that sex with Finn was no solution. Fortunately, the rational part of her was shouted down by her body, which was already thrilled at getting another chance to touch him, to feel him pressed against her. And her heart... well, she didn't want to think about what her heart was feeling.

"Come on," he said, leading her to the plane's cozy bedroom. They could touch the opposite sides of the room with their hands if they stretched, she noticed, but they only reached for each other. Instead of a furious mating, the way they had done it every time prior, this was unspeakably gentle. He took off her blouse, stroking her shoulders, kissing the side of her breast and the curve of her throat, the hollow of her collarbone. She shivered as his fingers traced down her hip, stroking over her pubic bone, smoothing around her belly. She let him peel off her slacks, shimmying out of her panties until she was naked and her skin felt fevered compared to the cool, temperature-controlled cabin air.

She took off his shirt, then stripped him out of his jeans. She started off slowly, kissing his chest, wanting to memorize every ridge of muscle, loving the way he jumped and danced beneath her fingertips. He growled as she traced a swirling path down his torso with her tongue. Her fingers dipped lower, finding his hardness.

He was large, hard, silky. His cock strained against her palm as she stroked him with a tentative hand.

She'd never wanted anyone as much as she wanted this man.

She took him into her mouth. His low, drawn-out groan of pleasure was music to her ears.

She moved slowly up and down his shaft, taking him in as deeply as she could. She could see his fists bunching into the comforter, heard his ragged breathing. She swirled her tongue around the head of his cock, tracing the tiny fissure there. She laved him lovingly, wanting to give him as much pleasure as he'd always given her.

It wasn't long before she heard him say, *"Diana."* And he dragged her up, kissing her, pulling her body against his. His body next to hers had her trembling, clinging to him.

"Now," she breathed urgently. "Please. I need you inside me now."

He reached over the side of the bed, producing a condom from his jeans. He rolled it on, then guided her above him. He teased her entrance, and she could feel him testing her, stroking her sensitive folds until she was panting with desire. She forced her way down, impaling herself on his throbbing cock. She gasped as he filled her, feeling his pulse between her thighs, deep inside her very core.

"Oh, Finn," she murmured, arching her back, taking him in deeper. She felt him shudder, heard him groan again with pleasure as he held her still and yet encouraged her to continue.

He let her set the pace, and she did, with slow, maddening strokes, each ending with her thrusting down on him as far as possible. She whispered, *yes,* every time his cock hit that special spot.

"You're driving me crazy," he said, his eyes closed, his face tight with strain.

She was driving them both crazy—and she was loving every second of it.

Finally, she couldn't take the building pressure anymore. Her measured strokes were growing more insistent. His hands gripped her thighs, his hips straining to meet her, and she drove herself downward, almost on the brink of sheer bliss. The orgasm shimmered through her, and she tossed her head back, crying out as she felt his cock jerk and shudder. She and Finn trembled together, clutching each other tightly.

When the moment had ended, they discovered their arms and legs were wound around each other. "I really care about you, Finn," she breathed, before pressing tiny kisses on his chest. "But I owe your family so much."

"Hush, baby. I know."

"What am I going to do?"

He didn't answer because he had no idea. All he knew was, she was tearing herself apart, and he had no damned solution for either of them.

FINN HAD INSISTED ON accompanying her to Thorn's office. Since it was technically the end of the bet, Diana supposed Thorn wouldn't see there was anything strange about Finn's presence. In fact, he'd probably have insisted on it. He'd want to start negotiating the terms of Finn's employment immediately. She'd already okayed the bills for Finn's refurbished office, his letterhead, his business cards. She figured as far as Thorn was concerned, this was an uncontested triumph. For the first time, he had his son right where he wanted him.

Or so he thought.

Diana flinched, but stepped away before Finn could comfort her. She shook her head.

"Not here in the hallway," she whispered. When his face clouded with hurt, she said, "I'll lose it, Finn. I'll break down, and I..."

To her horror, her voice cracked. She waited for a second, calming herself, taking several deep breaths.

"Just not here," she repeated, and was grateful when he nodded, understanding. She wasn't sure how this would play out. Thorn was waiting for them in his office. It was mostly floor-to-ceiling glass windows, with a glamorous view of the city and bay. A sumptuous Oriental rug covered the floor. The rest of the space was decorated with lots of modern touches. Clean, sharp, sophisticated: the room was all business. Thorn waited behind his glass desk, eyeing them as they walked in together. He was wearing a black suit and a blinding white shirt, with a blood-red silk tie. It was the power suit he wore when he was going to kick ass. Usually, it meant he was tearing apart a company, or reaming a failing organization before firing its management team.

The fact that he was wearing it now, for this occasion, both puzzled and unnerved her. His matching funereal expression only made matters worse.

"Son," Thorn said, barely glancing at Finn.

"Hey, Dad." Finn sounded subdued. "Listen, I wanted to—"

"A minute, Finn." His father cut across Finn's words as if they were some insubordinate flunky's, causing Diana's eyes to widen in shock. He'd sometimes been curt, often been frustrated, but this was strangely rude.

Then she saw the sheer fury in Thorn's eyes.

What the hell's happened since I've been gone?

"Some disturbing things have come to my attention while you two have been traipsing around on this Player's Club business," Thorn said, each word sharp enough to shred tin. "Very disturbing."

"Dad, what are you talking about?" Finn interrupted, before she could. He sounded defensive…and a little nervous. Neither was helping any, she noted.

Thorn stared at them both, then shrugged. "Fine. We'll do this your way. What do you have to report, then? How did your little 'experiment' go, Diana?"

She took a deep breath. "I…I found that the Player's Club… I found it…"

How can I do this? How can I not *do this?*

What do I do?

"She's ruling with you," Finn said, and all the breath seemed to leave her body as if she'd had the wind knocked out of her. "You were right the whole way. I'll go along with the plan."

"Finn, no," she said quickly, putting a hand on his arm.

His eyes revealed his determination. "Di, it's not that bad, really. You love this job."

"But you love the Club!"

He smiled, then shrugged. "Loves change."

Her heart warmed, and she stared at him, stunned.

Then she heard the loud sound of hands clapping slowly. She stared at Thorn, mocking them with his drawn-out applause.

"Bravo. Did you practice all of that, or were you improvising?"

"Dad, for god's sake, tell us what's happened?"

"I just wanted to see how far you'd take this charade, and I have to say, I'm disgusted with the pair of you."

"Charade?" Diana echoed, baffled. "Thorn, I can assure you, we didn't plan any of this. We didn't plan anything."

"I find that very hard to believe." He opened a manila envelope, tossed the contents on the broad surface of his desk.

Finn and Diana stepped up to examine the documents. There were pictures of them. At Disneyland. In Colorado. There they were in grainy black-and-white in the hotel in Anaheim, and their disheveled appearance was captured getting off the plane from Paris. The photos clearly showed that they were lovers, even though they weren't graphic.

"That wasn't planned, either," Diana said coldly. "And it doesn't..." She stopped to reconsider her words. "Actually, it has everything to do with why I wasn't going to agree with you about the bet. Thorn, the Player's Club isn't a dangerous organization. Finn might have some thrill issues—" she smiled as she said it "—but it's not the Club's fault. If anything I can see how liberating some might find it."

"I'm sure you could," Thorn snapped, and she felt guilty. How would she feel if her employee slept with her son? She couldn't fathom it.

"Finn, that was a nice little speech you gave, too. Very impassioned. But tell me, did you decide to bite the bullet because she's that good in the sack? Or because she made you feel bad because she knows she's going to get fired?"

Finn jolted and his fists clenched. "That's out of line, Dad. My relationship with Diana has nothing to do with you. If you're unhappy, it has to do with you, and how you do business."

"You're absolutely right there, my boy," Thorn said, his tone harsh. "Oh, and I suppose you'll make some grand gesture now, like throw away your board position, or take a vow of poverty."

"You keep it up and I might." Finn seemed equal parts pissed and puzzled. "*What is wrong with you?* Does my life bother you that much? Is it because Diana and I found each other during all of this? Or is it because she doesn't want to toe your line and let you railroad me into a life I'd hate?"

"You say you'd hate it, but you were about to accept it," Thorn shot back. "Tell me honestly. Is it because you care about her? That much?"

Finn looked at her, then nodded. "Absolutely."

Thorn stared daggers at her. "Damn you, Diana."

Finn stepped between them. "All right, that's enough. You've gone too far."

But his father only rounded the huge glass desk and shook his fist at her. "Did you really have a grand plan all along? Or were you going to slowly work your way up to sabotaging me? Was Finn part of it? Or have you been working with this damned Club?"

"*What* are you talking about?" Diana sputtered. She'd seen Thorn mad at times, even completely unreasonable; she'd just never seen either directed at her. "I'm sure it's upsetting to find out we're...involved. But this is beyond even your normal rage. What's really bothering you?"

"Diana, you're fired. And I'm sorry I ever agreed to take you on."

She felt his words like knives in her chest. Finn's protests sounded like a weak buzzing noise—the room suddenly seemed very far away, and she became lightheaded. "What?"

"You can't do this!" Finn shouted. "You can't fire her just because we slept together! You can't fire her because we fell in love!"

"I'm not," his father yelled. "I could kill her for hurting you...if she got you involved in any of this... but I'm not firing her for it."

He turned to her, his face a mask of contempt.

"I'm firing you," he said calmly, "because you embezzled one million dollars."

12

FINN STARED AT HIS FATHER as if he'd grown another head. "She what?"

"She stole from me. Stole from us," he corrected, and he actually bared his teeth. He seemed ready to lunge at Diana. "After I trusted you, Diana. Hell, after all Macalister Enterprises has done for you. How could you do this to us?"

"I...I didn't..." She could hardly speak; she was floored. "I didn't embezzle!"

"Of course she didn't!" Finn retorted. "Dad, have you gone crazy?"

"There's a paper trail, Diana. You're the one who was supposed to investigate this, and conveniently, it gets buried." A vein throbbed in his father's forehead—Finn was familiar with it, since it often showed up when his father chewed him out. It was weird not to be on the receiving end of that anger...and in this case, it was somehow worse. "I've got our comptroller tracing the accounts that are in your name. There's at least one dummy corporation siphoning large funds."

Diana stared at him. She felt shattered. "Do you really believe I'm capable of this, Thorn?"

"I've seen the evidence!"

Now she took a step toward him. "*Do you believe* I'm capable of this? Of betraying you and Macalister this way?"

"You have, damn it!" his father roared. "I thought taking you out of that awful family of yours would make a difference, but I guess the apple doesn't fall far from the tree, huh?"

Diana reeled back as if he'd belted her.

Finn started to speak, but his father interrupted.

"Don't you defend her, Finn. Don't you *dare* defend her."

"Will the police be charging me?" Diana said, her voice subdued. She could not look Thorn in the face.

"Once we gather the rest of the evidence, you bet your ass," Thorn growled. "In the meantime, you're out of here. Security will escort you out of the building."

"Are you serious?" Finn asked, incredulously.

"Fine." Diana walked to the door where a twenty-something security guard with a pimpled face was waiting. Finn followed her.

"Di…"

"You. Stay here," his father barked.

"Stay," Diana echoed weakly. "I'm fine."

"No, you're not."

"I will be." Her voice sounded hollow and raw. She left, and the door shut softly behind her.

Finn spun to confront his father. "If you actually believe this, you are out of your mind. She would rip off her own arm before she stole money from here, and you ought to know that."

"Shut up, Finn."

"You don't listen to me!"

"When a man thinks with his dick, then he doesn't really have a lot to offer the conversation, now, does he?" his father said. "And how do I know you're not in on this?"

Finn shook his head, starting to laugh. "Really? Are you serious? *Really?*"

His father's eyes burned like phosphorous. "Finn, you've been upset with me for trying to stop you from doing all your 'fun stuff.' What's to stop you from getting a little payback on your old man?"

Just as he was about to make a comment about his father's paranoia and insanity, some other part of him stopped him from reacting and forced him to truly look at his dad. "I've never seen you like this, with someone else."

"What?" His father slammed his hand on the desktop. "You've never seen me pissed? Never..."

"No," Finn countered quietly. "Hurting."

His father stopped abruptly, then scowled. "I'm not hurt, son, she's not worth it. Hell, I'm not even disappointed. I should've known this would happen."

"Why?"

"Because she was too damned perfect. You've seen how easily I go through employees. For her to last this long she had to have been planning this for years." He shook his head, and Finn saw from his body language that he was practically shaking. He sat down in his office chair. "I should've been more prepared."

"Did it ever occur to you that because you expect the worst, the worst tends to happen?" Finn was surprised that he could be this controlled. "I don't agree with what you did to Diana. I know for a fact that she didn't steal a dime from you. And I'm more than a little surprised that you're buying it."

"There's evidence, Finn," his father repeated. "You're too naive. You don't understand business. Or even things like evidence, apparently."

"I understand that you don't have enough for the police to be waiting here, instead of our own security," Finn said, and his father glared at him. "That means you don't have an ironclad case. Did it ever occur to you that she might have been set up?"

"Who would set her up?"

"I don't know. She's the one you call the Hammer, isn't she? I'm sure she's annoyed or ticked off lots of people. And maybe someone just wants to take your head lawyer and adviser away from you," Finn said.

His father was still scowling, but there was an added grudging acknowledgment, as well...and a touch of respect. "You sound awfully logical. That her doing?"

Finn couldn't but grin, albeit without the humor. "You know, I think it is."

"Too bad." His father shook his head, ran his hands over his face. "It's done. Unless she can prove that she's innocent, she's out of a job and she's got a criminal investigation heading her way. Period."

"She'll beat it. I know it."

Finn started to turn and leave, to look for her, when his father stopped him. "Finn, I've still got the details that Diana dug up, that leverage she had to get you out of the Club," he added. "And I will use it, Finn. Make no mistake, I'll use it."

Lincoln's financials. *Shit.*

"If you do, Dad, then you're not going to see me again. Period." Finn glanced over his shoulder. "I'm not bluffing here."

With that, he walked out. He would be with Diana as soon as he could, but first he had to take care of her—and the Club. As he sprinted down the hallway, he hit a speed-dial number on his cell phone.

"Hey, Finn," Lincoln said easily. "How was Paris?"

"Later," Finn interrupted. "We've got an emergency. You're going to have to mobilize people, because...well, there's something bad you need to know."

DIANA SAT AT HOME in a daze. After Thorn's shocking allegation, all she wanted to do was run from the Macalister building. She couldn't bear to face her assistant Penny's expression, couldn't bear to have all her coworkers watching as she was frog-marched away with her paltry personal items in a cardboard box. She'd fled directly to her car, and driven home carefully, gripping the steering wheel tightly enough so that her hands stopped shaking.

She hadn't cried. At least she'd saved herself that one shred of dignity.

Now, she just felt...lost. What was she supposed to do? Macalister was the only place she'd worked since she graduated law school. The only place she'd thought about working, honestly, and now, she'd ruined it. Not only would she not get a good reference, at this rate she was looking at jail time. Who hired a lawyer who had been to jail?

Other than my family, anyway.

Quickly, she tucked her head between her knees, breathing deeply because again she felt light-headed. God, what was she going to do?

There was a knock on her door. *Please, not the police,* she thought. She wasn't ready. She didn't know how to face this, who to turn to.

"Diana, it's Finn."

She opened the door cautiously.

"I tried calling you," he said, his eyes full of sympathy. "But your phone was shut off."

"Company phone," she said. Her tongue felt thick. "They would have closed the account. Protocol."

It was ironic. Stupid, but also ironic.

She glanced past Finn. He wasn't alone. Just beyond him on the sidewalk were a few others: Lincoln she recognized, and the stunning brunette with him, Juliana Mayfield. And Amanda, the silvery-blond-haired pledge, and Scott, and...Tucker, she seemed to remember.

"What are they doing here?" Did he really think that a Player's Club outing would solve *this* problem?

Finn's chin took on that determined jut that she'd gotten so used to seeing. "They're here because they want to help."

She laughed in shock. "Oh, yeah. Sure they do."

"I assure you," Lincoln put in, his intense look at odds with his mild tone, "I'm all about helping you out right now."

She winced. He knew, she thought. It was obvious Finn had told him she'd dug into his financial records. And he looked plenty pissed about it.

"I imagine you'd like to help me right into jail," she murmured, staring at Finn. She wasn't prepared for this, either, although it was better than the police showing up. Still, she wasn't equipped to deal with the Player's Club either.

Finn brought her inside, motioning to the others to stay back.

"True. It's in Lincoln's best interest that you get cleared," Finn admitted. There was a grim note to his voice that suggested he'd done a lot of persuading to get this rescue crew together. "Cleared, you can make sure that the stuff you collected about him is destroyed. He's going to need the name of that private investigator, too."

Personal interest. Now that, she understood. In a weird way, she trusted it more than talk of any brotherly love altruism.

Still.... "How can Lincoln help, Finn? How can any of them help?"

"Oh, you'd be surprised," he said, and he addressed the others. "Okay, let's move this along, people."

Diana watched, vaguely disconcerted, as they filed into her place. "You have a lovely home," Amanda said, giving her hand a squeeze, her expression sympathetic.

"Um, thanks," Diana said. "I...er, hired a decorator."

And wasn't that a lame thing to say, especially in these circumstances?

Juliana hung back as the rest moved to the living room. She put a hand on Diana's arm, too, holding her back. Her expression held no sympathy.

"If any of the information you dug up on Lincoln comes to light," Juliana said forcefully, "I'll bury you. Just thought you should know."

Diana stared at Juliana. "I don't blame you," she said. "It's no defense, but I was doing my job."

Juliana's smile was like a Cheshire cat's…sly, with the potential for viciousness. "How'd that work out for you?"

"Juliana." This from Finn, who had come back to see what was holding up Diana.

Juliana smiled brightly. "Only a little girl talk, Finn," she purred, but her gaze was still lethal.

Finn sighed, then put a protective arm around Diana.

"I still don't see how you guys think you can fix this," Diana said, as he led her into the living room, sat down next to her on the couch.

"We're a creative bunch of people," Tucker said, then surprised her by blowing a large, purple gum bubble. "And we've got some experience in some weird areas."

"Like what?"

The bubble popped, and he continued chewing contentedly. "I'm pretty good with computers."

"Considering he made his first million by the time he was thirteen because of the computer programs and internet protocols he developed, I'd say that's a bit of an understatement," Finn explained.

Lincoln cleared his throat. "As you no doubt put together, I've had some experience with things that bent the law a bit."

"We're like a really fun criminal think tank," Juliana interjected, leaning against Lincoln, who automatically wrapped an arm around her waist.

"Criminal." The word rasped from her throat. Diana shot Finn an anxious look. "What exactly are we talking about here? What do you think you're going to do?"

"We're not really *breaking* the law, per se," Finn said.

She covered her eyes with the heels of her palms. "Finn, I'm a lawyer, remember? Who comes from a criminally active family? I know the difference between bending and breaking."

"All right. We're probably more breaking than bending," Finn conceded. "But…"

"Funny to hear a sudden attack of conscience from you, Diana," Lincoln said, before Finn could finish. "Considering what we're proposing is no more illegal than what you've done by researching my financial information."

Everyone else, except Juliana, looked away for a minute as an awkward tension descended.

"Lincoln," Diana said, interrupting the silence. "I can't tell you how sorry I am for that. I don't know how I can make up for that…short of saying that, if I go ahead with this, I'll make sure that your information is destroyed. And I'll make sure my private investigator has no records, either."

Lincoln nodded.

Diana hid her face with her hands for a second. To prove she hadn't broken the law, she was going to have to...break the law.

It felt as if she were spitting on the very reason she'd become a lawyer. But Thorn hadn't hired her because of her ethics—he'd hired her for her unflinching willingness to get into the trenches and carry out his orders. She'd thought she was doing something good, but the bottom line was, she went places other lawyers wouldn't go—put up with more than any of them would—and that's why she was still at Macalister. She'd done it out of a misguided sense of loyalty, and had assumed that the loyalty went both ways.

She was wrong. And now, she was mad.

"All right," she said.

"All right." Finn rubbed his hands together, but Lincoln held his hand up.

"One last question," Lincoln said. "Did you steal the money?"

"No," Diana said. She looked Lincoln directly in the eye. "No, I did not."

He stared for a long minute, then he nodded.

"Just like that?" she asked in disbelief. Thorn, who had known her for years, hadn't accepted her denial... and she hadn't dug into *his* financial dirty laundry. "You believe me?"

"You're not lying," Lincoln said. "I might not trust you, but on this, at least, I can tell you're being straight."

The relief she felt was overwhelming, and she felt tears prick her eyes. "It's not going to be easy," she said, surreptitiously wiping away the moisture with the back of her hand. “In fact, I think it’s going to be impossible.”

“Not to worry,” Finn said. “The impossible’s my favorite.”

13

"To our success, boys!"

George was at his small, bland town house, popping the cork on champagne and letting some of the frothing mass spill out onto the ugly rented carpet. These surroundings wouldn't be his for much longer, he thought, filling the three crystal flutes.

Jonesy shook his head. "Nah, that's a woman's way to toast," he said, holding up his squat square glass of whiskey. "Maybe that's more Vic's drink, eh? With a maraschino cherry in it?"

As Jonesy laughed, Victor, wearing a green walking cast on his left leg, didn't say anything, but eyed the man warily. Victor didn't touch his champagne.

"Now, now, play nice." George hated the fact that he, too, was nervous around Jonesy. "We pulled it off, didn't we? It's all settled. We've got the money, Diana's catching the blame for it, and Finn and his dad are on the outs. The way it'll play out, Finn'll quit voluntarily, because he's an idiot. So let's not focus on the...previous unpleasantness."

"Easy for you to say," Victor muttered. "It's not your leg that psycho broke."

Jonesy's eyes gleamed. "Be thankful, yeah?" he said, running his tongue around his teeth. "It could've been your right leg—at least you can drive." His smile was fierce. "And it could've been worse even than that, Vic. Much, much worse."

Victor didn't say anything else.

"You've got your cut, Jonesy," George pointed out. "So I guess you're on to bigger and better things. You going to use that quarter mil to start getting your own revenge?"

"What revenge?" Jonesy said.

George stared for a second. "You know. On your family." He waited a beat as Jonesy simply looked at him blankly. "They cut you out of your family fortune, and you said that you were going to use the money to get some payback, make some money while you're at it. They're in, what, London?"

Jonesy's laughter was loud, almost infectious—George might've joined him, if he hadn't seen the cold glint behind in the man's eyes.

"Good grief, you're like a toddler. Sure I told you that, mate. It's what you wanted to hear…no, it's what you *needed* to hear right then, wasn't it?"

George frowned. "You only…said it to make me feel better?"

"You are seriously stupid," Jonesy marveled. "I couldn't have run the con otherwise, could I?"

George went cold. "This…"

"Worked better than I would've expected for something I came up with on the fly," Jonesy said, preening. "I heard you complaining to everyone about what you were owed, and found out just how close you were to the Macalister money. Easy enough from there to do a little researching and a little planning. Then all I had to do was buy you a drink, tell you a sob story, and wait for you to roll over. Child's play. You were easier than a ten-dollar whore, Georgie."

Temper burned through George, hot enough to have him swinging at Jonesy. He'd already started drinking, though, and Jonesy dodged his clumsy roundhouse punch, before delivering a harsh blow of his own. Suddenly, George was on the ground, clutching at his side, straining for his next breath. He stared up at Jonesy through eyes that watered.

"Let's not do that again, eh?" Jonesy sounded bored. "Getting your ass kicked won't change the situation, after all."

"So you conned me for a quarter of a million." George closed his eyes. He ought to just pretend it was a finder's fee, he thought. Look at Jonesy as a consultant, some kind of coach. Yeah. That way it was an operating expense…and not that he was a complete and utter idiot.

"Now, that's a bit of a misstatement," Jonesy said, and he seemed genuinely cheerful. "The quarter mil was a very nice start. But here's where the deal sweetens."

He towered over George, and George had to force himself not to cower.

"The way I see it, if everything works out, you'll be coming into some steady money, Georgie boy, and our gambling friend Victor here will no doubt be promoted for his diligence, which will mean a small increase in his income, as well. Since we both know he shouldn't be trusted with more money, I can't see why I shouldn't get that increase, plus a bit more. It'd probably be in your best interest to keep me in the lifestyle I'm now accustomed to."

"Why should I?" George spluttered.

"Well, two reasons, really," Jonesy said pleasantly. "The first being that neither of you would like the details of this little scenario known, not by your uncle, and certainly not by the police."

George felt his cheeks flush, his eyes water with anger more than pain now.

"And here's the second."

He delivered a swift kick to George's stomach, and he let out a muffled scream.

"Get up and drink your girlie drink, Georgie," Jonesy said cruelly, heading for the door. "Because I don't know how much you'll feel like celebrating for a good long while."

FINN WOKE UP in Diana's bed, with the sun streaming in through a high window. She was a morning person, he thought groggily. God save him from morning people.

She rolled over, and her lush naked skin was next to him. Now there was a whole new side to morning that he could appreciate.

He stroked her hair over one shoulder, pressing intent kisses against her neck, down her spine. She was backing her pert ass against his rock-hard erection. "Good morning," he said huskily, reaching around and cupping her breast as his cock teased at her thighs.

She glanced at him over her shoulder. "I can't believe you're here." Her brown eyes were as rich as Parisian hot chocolate. "Can't believe we're here together."

He smiled. "I know exactly how you feel."

"How?" she murmured, so softly that he barely heard her. "You're rich, good-looking. You could have any woman you want."

"I've never wanted any woman the way I want you," he responded. She was such a puzzle. She was the only thing that stirred him as much as his crazy stunts had. "You don't see how special you are, Diana. But I do."

She turned around, crushing her breasts against his chest. "Kiss me, Finn."

"Absolutely," he answered, and did as she requested. The kiss was a slow exploration, like someone returning to a favorite spot after years of yearning absence. He tasted her, leisurely, his tongue tracing the soft inner skin of her lips until she shivered against him. Then he coaxed her tongue to do the same. When she did, it was as if his body exploded…he wanted all of her, all at once.

Slow down, he chastised himself. He didn't need to be in any rush. He had years, a lifetime, to touch and tempt her.

Wait a second. Years?

Before he could examine that new thought too closely, she sighed against him. Her hand smoothed a path up his chest, her rounded nails clawing delicately along his abs, causing him to shudder. When her fingers circled his shaft, milking him with gentle pressure, he leaned his head against her shoulder, knowing he'd lost control.

He couldn't slow down now for anything or anyone.

He cupped her breasts, and she arched her back, filling his palms with her, moaning softly in the back of her throat. He groaned in response, his cock hardening painfully, wanting her damp, hot passage. He leaned down, sucking her nipple gently between his lips, and he let his teeth grate softly over it, gratified by her gasp. He reached down, still suckling, his fingers pushing aside the small tangle of curls to discover she was ready, causing his body to tense even more. He pressed a finger past her folds, finding the hard, throbbing nubbin of flesh. He traced it tenderly, feeling her buck slightly beneath his hand.

"Finn," she sighed, her breathing shaky. He pressed his finger in deeper, relishing the rippling texture of her tight heat. He groaned, wanting nothing more than to press even deeper, with more than his fingers. Instead, he added a second finger, pressing inside her and withdrawing rhythmically as he sucked on first one nipple, then the other.

She was arched beneath him like a bow, her hips urging him on. He had her wet and moaning, her head moving back and forth restlessly. Then he paused, causing her to complain in a wordless cry.

He reached for a condom from the nightstand, rolling it on as fast as if his life depended on it.

He was on top of her now, and she wrapped her legs around his waist, tightly. "Now, Finn," she pleaded, her voice drenched with urgency.

He eased forward, made easier by her slickness even as her body welcomed him. "Diana," he groaned, shuddering slightly, forcing himself to hold perfectly still for fear of losing control in one split second.

She leaned up, nipping at his collarbone. He savored the feel of her body surrounding him. He pushed on. She met each slow thrust with a sweet pressure of her own. He kept up the rhythm, a slow, steady beat of intensity and longing.

She was panting in harsh, choppy breaths, and her body gripped him. His thrusts more eager, more intense.

"Finn!" she screamed, surprising him, and her body contracted hard. His orgasm, likewise, hit him hard, surprising him yet again, and he yelled as he came.

"I like waking up with you," he said, and she let out a ringing burst of laughter.

"You're better than an alarm clock," she teased him right back. "Want to take a shower?"

They did, and he wound up deciding to repeat the performance, only wet and vertical. And then there was a bout on the washing machine, where she wrapped her legs around his waist as the vibration of the dryer sped them on to completion.

By lunchtime, he was worn out.

"We've got to stop this," Diana said, with a breathless chuckle, as they headed for the kitchen. "I know you're trying to keep my mind off my problems, but if you cheer me up any more, I don't think I'm going to be able to walk!"

"We need sustenance," he announced. "Maybe some water. Vitamin C."

"I'll see if anybody delivers oysters," she said, with a saucy wink.

He smiled, then heard his phone ringing. His father. He glanced at Diana, who was humming happily and going through take-out menus near the phone. "I've got to answer this," he said, hoping his smile didn't look too fake as he slipped out the back door and took the call. "Dad."

"Glad you're picking up." His father's voice was tense. "Son, I didn't want it to come to this. Not any of it."

"Dad, unless you've got something new to tell me, or you're going to apologize and give Diana her job back… well, I don't see what else we have to talk about."

"I'm not losing this one." He could almost hear his father's molars grinding together. "I'm not going to lose *you*. Not to some brainwashing thrill cult and not to an embezzling whore."

Finn clicked off the phone. It rang again, shrilly, and Finn let it ring. He stood on Diana's back porch, fuming.

He knew, somehow, that his father loved him. At moments like this, he could have done with less love.

Finally, there was the beep that told him his father had texted him. He glanced at it…then stopped. It didn't say anything obscene or redundant. It had just four words.

Check your bank balance.

He felt his stomach knot. He wouldn't.

Quickly, Finn used his phone to call up his bank accounts.

Empty. All of them.

"What the hell?" He dialed his banker's private number.

"Finn, I'm sorry," his banker, Frank, said without even so much as a hello.

Finn's spirit fell further. "He can't *do* this, Frank."

"The money from the malpractice lawsuit… Technically, his name was still on the account. Your parents turned it over to you, but…"

"I'm the one who almost died!"

"Yeah, but they were the ones footing the medical bill. It's a gray area."

Finn growled. "The trust fund. Grandma Amelia's. It wasn't much, but…"

"Your father's contesting the will and your feasibility to manage it. He didn't take the money, but it is frozen."

Finn blinked. "What about…" Jeez, what about what? "What does that leave me?"

"Right now, not much." At least he sounded apologetic. "I would've fought him, but he's one of my biggest clients."

"I'm getting that a lot." Grim resolve was like a frozen fist against his chest.

"I don't suppose you know a lawyer that would work for cheap?" Frank asked.

Finn smiled. "Strangely enough, I've got one that might help—but I don't think it'll come to that. Thanks, Frank." He hung up, shaking with anger and confusion.

His father was playing hardball. He'd heard about his father's invasive modus operandi in business, about his high-handed and manipulative tactics. He'd never thought Thorn would stoop so far with his own son.

He walked back into the house.

"Do you like Greek food? I was thinking..." She stopped when she saw his face. "What happened?"

"Nothing."

She went to him, framing his face in her hands. "Don't lie to me."

"How can you tell?" he said, bargaining for time.

She smiled weakly. "Because that's what my face looked like when your father fired me."

He told her everything...the bank accounts, the threats, the whole nine yards. She accepted it all with a stoic face.

"He's been planning this," she said. "He kept the contingencies in place just in case."

"Damn it. I guess I should have seen that, but..."

"But you didn't want to believe it." Diana nodded. "Believe me, I know."

"So. I guess I'm, er, broke." He laughed, then a thought struck him. "Jeez. What'll happen to my house?"

"Don't worry about it right now," Diana counseled. "We'll talk to the Club. They're your friends. They'll want to help you."

Finn felt so helpless. So furious. But he didn't know what else to do.

14

THEY DIDN'T WASTE ANY TIME. They decided on Tucker's loft once they'd settled on the details of the plan. They were going to hack into the computers at Macalister Enterprises and from there they'd trace how the embezzling had happened, how the frame had been constructed. And they'd find the files that held Lincoln's personal information and delete any trace of it.

"Is that all?" Tucker asked, almost gleefully, at her house. "Because I can sneak in a virus if you want, clean Macalister's out. Hell, I could…"

"No," Diana and Finn had said together, and Tucker had grudgingly complied.

So now they were at Tucker's place. It was in an industrial district, and his seemed the only inhabited space, a loft with a unique dystopian feel that was a little creepy. Diana moved instinctively next to Finn. She hated this. She *hated* this.

"It'll be all right," Finn said, putting a protective arm around her after they stepped into the freight elevator. As it bumped and screeched its way to the loft, Finn leaned down, pressing a gentle but thorough kiss against her lips, warming her from the inside out. She leaned into him.

"Finn," she breathed.

"Later, I promise. When this is all over, I'm going to do about a million different things to you and you won't even remember your name, much less what we had to do tonight." His voice was full of sexy promise. "So hang in there."

The elevator screeched to a halt, and Finn opened the door. Several other Players were there already, Diana noted. Juliana wasn't, though, nor was Amanda. There was a woman named Jackie who was apparently a new recruit. *A pledge,* she reminded herself, and she wondered what the woman's three challenges were. She didn't look as if she'd lived a life of regret, so what would she want to do before she died…

"All right," Tucker said, licking his lips and opening a liter bottle of Mountain Dew. He was wearing a T-shirt that said L33T—the cryptic, nerdy notation meaning *elite.* "The sitch. You're not under arrest or anything, right?"

"No." *Not yet,* the voice in her head said, and she forced herself not to focus on the sick feeling in the pit of her stomach.

"Why can't you just go to the police?" Jackie, the recruit, asked.

"I'm being set up," Diana answered. "Whoever's doing it is on the inside of the company, and now there's attention. They've got to cover tracks. They've got to finish the frame and hope it doesn't get discovered."

"You don't think that Macalister's accountants will figure out what's really going on?" Jackie pressed. "I mean, he's richer than God. I'm sure his money people are good and all."

"They are," Diana said. "Which is why I'm betting it's one of them."

That statement met only silence as its import sunk in.

"They'll fix things in a way that locks me in, and then eliminate all evidence that proves my innocence. By the time the police get a warrant—or were invited in—I'll be the only suspect."

Tucker cracked his knuckles. "Here's what we're going to do. You used to have a remote sign-in, right? A way to access your files online, no matter where you were?"

She nodded. "But they'll have shut that down, changed the passwords," she said, with a quick, bitter smile.

"You sure? That sort of thing takes time."

'It's standard procedure when somebody's terminated," she said. "I should know. I enacted it."

"Ouch." He nodded, then rubbed his hands together. "All right, then. Do you have anybody else's password?"

She hesitated, feeling awkward.

Tucker looked grim. "Diana, I think we're past all that, don't you?"

She nodded. "I remember my old boss's password.

It was before the standard procedure went into action, I think."

"It's a start," Tucker said absently. "All right. From here, we dig."

Tucker started the digging, and in what seemed like a ridiculously short time, he got in. Soon they were sifting through the computer's databases, looking for the information she'd gotten on Lincoln and the accounting files that were being used to frame her. Until they had those files, the real criminals wouldn't be caught.

She stared at what they were doing. *As opposed to the "fake" criminals, like you?*

She went to the kitchen to get a glass of water. Lincoln was already there, drinking a Bass ale, leaning casually against the countertop. His gaze chilled, and he began to leave.

"I'm sorry," she said softly. "That I pulled your financials. I thought, I mean, lots of people have Swiss bank accounts, and it looks like you were laundering money, but it's not my business. I've done shady things…"

"Like pulling my financials," Lincoln noted.

"And I said to myself as long as my work was involved, I was doing whatever I needed to for the only thing that mattered to me."

Lincoln took a deep breath. "The money is being laundered."

She blanched. "You don't have to tell me," she said. "In fact, really—don't tell me."

"It was from my father," he said. "He was a prominent politician. I was illegitimate. He and my mother never wanted the connection made public. That's the only reason for the secrecy."

"I'm sorry," she said.

"Don't be. Twelve years ago, more, I wasn't exactly walking the straight and narrow. Hung out with a bad crowd and learned a hell of a lot of bad things." He shrugged. "I stopped. You might say I channeled it into the Player's Club."

"Oh?"

He must've heard suspicion, because he shook his head. "We don't thrill seek for the hell of it. We sure as hell don't hurt people. And generally speaking, we don't break the law." He paused, then smiled. "Okay, there was the Mighty Mouse mural, and I wound up buying that anyway, so it's practically legal. And we did break into George's house that one time."

She choked.

"But that was to retrieve something he'd stolen, something he was planning on using to get a bunch of us into trouble," he pointed out. "Much like you're doing now. Call it self-defense."

"Self-defense," she mused, wondering if she believed it or simply liked the sound of it because it made her own position defensible.

He crossed his arms. "I was doing it to protect Juliana," he said. "I was doing it to protect Finn, and all these people I care about like family."

"Like a family." She couldn't keep the envy, or longing, out of her voice. "I can see why Finn fought tooth and nail to stay in."

Lincoln's expression softened slightly. "There's that.

But Finn wouldn't lose us if he'd just scale back his activities." He took a long pull from the beer bottle. "I think his father's a tough bastard—don't get me wrong—but Finn's been getting progressively more... Well, he's more of an extreme player in the Player's Club."

She tilted her head to one side. "You know why he does this," she said quietly, knowing how they started the Club. She was surprised to see the censure in his eyes.

"I didn't know you knew," he said, and it was as if some tension was released. "He must really trust you. He doesn't generally let anyone know about his past, or his..."

"Yes," she said, when he didn't finish the thought. "He trusts me."

Lincoln shifted his position, taking another sip of beer. "I love him like a brother," he said. "But I've been worried."

"Worried, why?"

"I don't suppose he told you about Everest."

"Everest?" She blinked rapidly. "As in, the mountain?"

Finn came in just then. "You okay?" he asked, looking pointedly at Diana.

"I'm fine," she said. "What's this about you going to Everest?"

Finn scowled. "Really, Linc? You brought that up *now?*"

"I didn't know you hadn't told her," Lincoln said

innocently. "You seem to have told her a lot of other things."

Diana crossed her arms.

"This is so not the right time," Finn pointed out with irritation. "After all this is over and things get back to normal, it'll be fine. Believe me. We'll talk about it then."

She took a deep breath, nodded. "People climb it every year," she said, still uncertain.

"People die on it every year," Lincoln added. "Especially when they haven't put in the proper training time."

"That's enough, Lincoln."

Lincoln shook his head. "I love you like a brother, and I thank God every day we started the Club," he said slowly. "You care a lot about her. I know it's fighting dirty...but if it means I don't spread your ashes over Kilimanjaro or wherever, then I'll deal the low blow, Finn."

With that, Diana watched as Lincoln rejoined the others.

She turned, staring at Finn. "Do you have a death wish?"

He looked tortured. "Diana," he whispered. "I don't... You wouldn't understand."

She held his face in her hands.

"We'll talk about it later," she promised, kissing him. "Or we won't. Don't worry about it now, okay?"

He seemed so thankful, her heart was breaking.

She loved him, so she would let him make that choice...even though it might kill her.

FINN DIALED Ben's number. Diana was busy with the Players. They'd found the financial information they were searching for, but they hadn't quite winnowed it down to who was behind it all yet. It would probably take hours more. Hell, possibly days. In the meantime, Finn had no money.

He'd always thought that money didn't matter to him, and technically, it didn't. It didn't matter if he lived in a swanky town house or shared an apartment with thirty guys—which, at this point, looked likely, he thought. It didn't matter if he had a BMW or a beat-up Chevy Nova. What did matter, though, were his adventures.

If he didn't have those, what else mattered? He shuddered, then got a grip when Ben answered the phone.

"Jeez, where have you been, man," Ben said, sounding disgruntled. "I've got a few other people interested in the Everest thing. And guess what?"

"Um, Ben." Finn tried to interrupt, but Ben was too hell-bent to notice.

"*Next week,* baby!" Ben hooted. "Tell me your passport's in order. I can even line up a doctor to give you the shots."

"What's the rush, Ben?" Finn asked, a little disgruntled himself by this point.

There was a pause on the other end of the line. "What do you mean? Why should I wait? Most pledges do their challenges in a month!"

"Yeah, but most pledges don't pick Everest, Ben," Finn shot back. "If you hurry, you can get hurt. You could get others hurt."

"I'm careful," Ben protested. "More careful than you. So if this is about you, and you're scared..."

"I'm not scared," Finn snapped. "I could do it tomorrow *if I had the damned money!*"

There. He'd said it.

"Whoa. Didn't know it was a money issue." Ben sounded subdued. "Huh."

"And with the hard-on you've got, I'm sure one hundred and fifty thousand or so isn't that big a deal...."

"More like two hundred," Ben corrected.

Finn winced. "Two hundred large. Right now I'm probably going to lose my condo and my car, so finding that kind of pocket change isn't really in the cards."

"Shit." Ben went silent for several seconds, then sighed. "Okay. Well, I've got a spare room."

Finn finally cracked a smile. "Great offer, but I think I've probably got that covered, actually."

"That woman problem straightened itself out, huh?"

"Something like that."

"Well, I don't have two hundred thousand lying around," Ben said. "Sorry about that."

"If you want to go without me, at least let me line up another Player to go with you...and check it out," Finn said, regret boring a hole in his chest. "I still want to go. It just looks like it's going to take me longer than I thought."

"Right," Ben said easily.

Finn paused. "You're still going, aren't you? Next week?"

"Yes." His tone was absolute.

"Why are you in such a hurry, Ben?" Finn asked.

The pause drew out interminably. Finally, Ben sounded weary. "Why'd you invite me to the Player's Club, Finn?"

"I don't know," Finn said, laughing. Then shrugged, even though Ben couldn't see it over the phone. "You reminded me of me, I guess."

"So why did you start the Club?"

Finn leaned back. He hadn't told his story to anyone for years, and now he was telling two people in a matter of a week. "I've got leukemia."

A startled silence this time. "Oh?"

"Almost died. Couple of times. It's in remission now," Finn said slowly, "but…"

"Yeah. I know." Ben's voice was a mere whisper. "I'm going blind, Finn."

Finn closed his eyes. "Oh," he echoed. The kid was only twenty. What had he seen by the time he was twenty? Not enough. Not enough by half, if he was going blind.

"Not for a while…but soon enough." Ben sounded grim—but determined. "It's degenerative, and fairly fast moving. If I'm not going to be able to see again, I'm going to damned well see everything I can."

"I wish to God I could go with you," Finn said, and meant it with every fiber of his being.

"Yeah, well, maybe we'll pass the hat." Ben's laugh was impossibly joyful, considering. "I'll talk to you soon."

Finn hung up, and then sat for a moment, hands in his pockets, eyes on the skyline.

Diana joined him on the sofa and rested her head

on his shoulder. Reflexively, he wrapped his arms around her.

"What are you thinking about?" she asked against his chest. "You look so sad."

"I just…I wonder what's the point sometimes. That's all."

"The Everest thing?"

He nodded. He didn't tell her about Ben going blind—didn't know if that was a secret he should share. But it ate at him.

"Finn, it'll be all right." She held him tight. "I promise, it'll be all right."

"I don't know how."

She smiled. "The guys found most of the info we needed, including Lincoln's file. It'll take some time to destroy his financial history. Let's go home."

"You mean your house?"

She nodded, then took him by the hand. "It can be your home as long as you want it to."

He drove them back, then followed her into her house, up to her bedroom. They made love, slowly, tenderly…with lots of deep, intense kissing. When his body joined with hers, he felt a sort of peace he hadn't ever known. He felt more alive than he could ever remember, too.

Afterward, in the darkness, he held her cradled against his chest, their heartbeats matching in time. "The Everest thing…"

"I told Ben I can't," he said. "He wants to go next week. I just can't afford that."

"How much is it?"

"Two hundred thousand."

She was quiet, and he felt sure he could hear her recriminations: *What sort of idiot pays that much money to do something that crazy? That dangerous? That...*

"I could give you the money."

"What?"

"I have savings," she said. "Macalister paid me well, and...other than the house, I don't really live all that extravagantly, and..."

"You'll need the savings," he said, feeling slightly ashamed. "I mean, I'm sure we can get this cleared up, but until then—"

"I've got a couple million," she said, shocking him even more. "If you really want to go, then you should go."

He sat up, staring at her in the dim light. He couldn't make out her expression. "I thought you'd be like Lincoln," he said eventually. "You know. Thinking I'm nuts. Thinking it's a death wish—like you asked."

"I hate it," she whispered. "The thought of you up there makes me break out into a cold sweat. But if it means that much to you, then you've got to do it."

"What if I died, Diana?"

"Then you'll die doing what you love."

He snuggled against her, holding her for a long time, thinking she'd fallen asleep. Until she spoke quietly in the darkness.

"Sometimes dying seems easier than living."

He squeezed her tight—and wondered if that was exactly what he was doing.

15

THE NEXT MORNING, Diana was hard at work analyzing the financial information copied from Macalister's. Tucker had covered his tracks, still, at some point she would have to reveal the fact that she'd hacked into the Macalister network to prove her own innocence.

At one time, Thorn would've looked at that and considered it moxie—the kind of take-no-prisoners, find-a-solution-at-any-cost mentality that he'd hired her for. Now he might simply suspect that she was covering up her own tracks and that her criminal blood was finally proving true. How could he trust her again?

Screw that. How could you trust him *again?*

She frowned as that thought crept to the forefront. No matter what else he'd done, she owed Thorn a lot. Her education. Her job experience.

You were a well-paid wage slave who put up with his temper and jumped through flaming hoops to keep him happy.

She quickly got up, started pacing. Where was all

this coming from? Had she had this resentment the whole time…or was it new and quickly spreading?

Could she get rid of it?

Did she want to?

She was still turning the matter over in her mind when Lincoln knocked on her home office door. "Finn let me in. He said that I could talk to you."

Lincoln still sounded reserved, even after their discussion in Tucker's kitchen. Though at least she felt as if they were on the same page, finally. She nodded, motioning him in.

He handed her a small sheaf of paper. "I took the liberty of going a few levels deeper," he said. "The guy we're looking for is somebody named Victor Sharonvsky. Somebody in the controller's office."

She frowned, trying to match a face to the name. "I've heard of him, but I'm not sure I've ever met him."

"I pulled his employee file, as well," Lincoln said, completely expressionless as he handed her another small pile of paper. "Seems clean as a whistle."

Her eyes narrowed. "So it seems." But something was off. She could feel it in the marrow of her bones.

"How far are you willing to go with this?" Lincoln asked.

She closed her eyes, knowing what he was asking. Would she be willing to bend the law again?

"I'm not like my family. I'm not stealing, I'm not hurting anyone. I'm not even 'following orders' this time. This is self-defense. If this is the guy framing me," she replied, "then all the way."

"Good." Lincoln pulled yet another sheet from the file. "I took the liberty and had his financials pulled."

She winced. "You didn't have to do that."

Lincoln waited until she met his gaze. "Yeah, I did," he said. "Because you're a Player now, and besides, you love Finn. Anybody who loves him is somebody I'm going out of my way to protect."

A moment of silent understanding passed between them. Then she took a quick glance at the papers. Her eyebrows rose.

"He's losing a lot of money," she murmured. "A lot, and regularly."

"I'd suspect gambling," Lincoln said. "With some digging I'm sure we can find out who he owes money to. It would make the most sense."

"Hmm." So she'd had her world destroyed because some idiot felt like betting on football, she thought. There were probably worse reasons, but she couldn't think of one offhand.

"I'll also bet that this wasn't his idea," Lincoln added. "Looking over Victor's employee file shows he doesn't have a background in computers, and while the job was a little sloppy, it was still conceived by someone who knows how to run this particular con."

"Sounds like you'd know," she retorted. "That's not a judgment, just an observation."

He shrugged. "I wasn't always a Player, Diana."

She let that stand. "All right. We'll get our hands on Victor. And when we do I think he'll be more than happy to sell out his partner."

Lincoln nodded. "You're tough," he said. "All right. Victor, here we come."

"Lincoln." He stopped abruptly and turned. "About Finn."

Lincoln glanced down the hallway. "I think he's on the phone with his lawyer. What's happening?"

"I actually understand how much this all means to him." Diana took a deep breath. "I've never felt this way before—with anyone. He's changed my life." She paused. "The Club has changed my life."

For the first time since she'd met him, a grin lit up Lincoln's face. He looked years younger, and almost incandescently happy. "That's what we do."

She smiled in response before she could stop herself. "He's convinced that the thrill of living life a certain way is what completes him." She bit her lip. " I want to know that."

"What are you saying?"

"Skydiving." Even the word made her clench her stomach. "I…I want to do that."

"Maybe you should do that with Finn," Lincoln said.

"Finn's so protective of me. I'd rather do this, and then tell him about it."

Lincoln smiled warmly. "You want to pull a Finn. Better to beg forgiveness…"

"Than ask permission," she finished, nodding. "Would you help me?"

Lincoln's grin widened. "It'd be my pleasure. About time somebody gave that kid a taste of his own medicine."

GEORGE CHECKED HIS WATCH for the time, then scowled at his buzzing phone, hoping against hope it wasn't Jonesy. Ever since the man—no, the *con artist*—had dropped his act and started demanding George pay him for keeping silent, George had been drinking steadily. He'd also started showing up late to work, and leaving early. Part of him wished he'd get fired: it would serve Jonesy right, wouldn't it?

Then he wondered what Jonesy might do if he couldn't come up with the payments he felt he deserved, and swallowed hard.

But it wasn't Jonesy. He answered the call with a growl. "Victor, what now?"

"I'm leaving town, George." Victor's voice shook. "If you were smart, you'd do the same."

"What?" George couldn't believe it. He straightened. The martinis he'd drunk as a sleep aid weren't working, only serving to slow down his thinking. "Leaving town? Why?"

"The con's falling through. Somebody's infiltrated the network and has been copying data. I'll bet it's that bitch Diana." Vic's voice was high-pitched and frightened. "The cops'll be onto us soon."

"Jonesy said that they probably wouldn't find out it was us," George said, his own voice starting to shake.

"He said that they wouldn't if they believed the evidence we planted," Victor countered, irritation creeping into his voice. "I *knew* we shouldn't have underestimated her. The police might not have dug deeper, but she got in, George. I don't know how, but she *did*."

"How do you know anybody did?" George asked sharply. *Please, please, let him be overreacting....*

"Because Jonesy had me add this thing that dinged a security alert if anyone other than me accessed the file with the evidence," Victor snapped. "And it looks like there were a few people who tried to get it until someone with high enough clearance was able to."

"So?" George gripped the phone tighter. "There's an open investigation."

"Yeah, well, the guy's account they hacked into hasn't worked in the company in nine years," Victor spat back. "And it was Diana's old boss...the lawyer before her, so the account had clearance. *And* she could've remembered the password!"

"Maybe...maybe somebody else..." George said, feeling less sure.

"Oh? And would that same someone make sure the file she'd marked as blackmail against Finn also mysteriously disappeared?"

George went hot with fury, then cold with realization.... "The Players. Finn drafted the Players."

"I don't know, and I don't care," Victor said. "But when it all comes out, I'll be in another country, George. And unless you're willing to roll over on that psycho pal, Jonesy, of yours, you should get a one-way ticket out of here."

"Grow a pair," George snorted. "This will all—"

"I've helped you as much as I can," Victor snarled. "I shouldn't have bothered." And he hung up.

George flung the phone against a wall, watching

as the expensive model bounced on the ground. He stomped it a few times for good measure.

Then, slowly, he started to get his bearings…and realize just what sort of mess he was in.

Victor was right. Jonesy complicated everything. Even if—and the thought had him queasy—even if he took the rap and went to jail, Jonesy would still be ticked that he didn't have the money he was expecting.

Maybe Jonesy wouldn't think jail was punishment enough.

Grimacing, George went to his house phone, dug up Jonesy's number.

"George," Jonesy answered, sounding amused and a little bored. "Not calling to beg, are you? I hate hearing a man beg."

"There's a problem." As fast as he could, he told Jonesy what Victor had told him. "What are we going to do?"

Jonesy was silent for a long, tense minute. "This has been a cock-up from day one," he spat. "I suppose our rabbit Victor is already on the run."

George froze, as if unsure. Victor had already had his leg broken. What else was Jonesy capable of?

"No, no, that's fine," Jonesy said, his voice almost soothing. "As it happens, I figured he'd choose that route. Why else'd I break his leg? He's more scared of me than the police, and too right, he should be. But his running works into my plan."

George goggled. "What are you talking about?"

"Running makes a person look guilty. Cops may think he's in it with her, or behind it on his own,"

Jonesy explained, as if a child should have figured it out. "It's inconvenient that it's shaking out this way, but there it is."

George frowned. "So, we don't have to worry that Diana and Finn are the ones digging into this?"

"Listen, it's in my best interest to make sure you stay off the hook and get that fancy-pants, high-paying board position," he said. "It'll either be Diana on the hook for this, or Victor, or the both of them. Don't worry."

"And if they dig deeper?" He didn't know what sadistic streak made him push Jonesy this way, but he was tired of being treated like an idiot.

"They won't."

"But how can you be *sure?*"

"You really want to know the details? Now?" Jonsey's tone took on a more sinister edge. "Well, then, I've been having that bitch lawyer followed, haven't I. I can't imagine why she'd consider skydiving now, since so many accidents have been known to happen."

A chill traveled up George's spine.

"If anything were to happen to her, I imagine the police would definitely suspect Victor of tying up loose ends," he said.

George was stunned. "Wait. What?"

"With both of them gone and Finn no longer in the picture, you'll find the avenue cleared for promotion. And you're going to be pushing plenty of cash at me to cover…well, some unexpected expenses."

George gripped the counter of his wet bar. "You're talking about murder."

Jonesy hissed. "You're on an open phone line, Georgie, so watch yourself. I'm just conjecturing." He paused. "Be careful. It's a dangerous world out there."

He hung up.

George placed the phone in its cradle, then slid down the wall until his backside hit the floor.

He'd always wanted what Finn had. Just wanted what Georgie deserved.

How did I get here, instead?

16

"I CAN'T BELIEVE THEY didn't tell me," Finn groused to himself, shifting his car into fifth and zooming toward the airfield.

He'd spent the morning talking with his accountant about cutting back on his expenses, and with his lawyer, since they'd all need a really good one once this was over. So today he was particularly annoyed. He didn't want to miss Diana's first jump.

He knew that she was becoming more open to the Player's Club, since he'd explained why he started it. He was sure she was scared, and wished that she'd chosen to skydive with him. Why hadn't she told him?

Or maybe she'd just tried to reconcile with Lincoln; he was still pretty mad that she'd had him investigated. He frowned. He doubted that, though. And again, why wouldn't she have told him?

Maybe she's trying to impress you? Maybe she wants to surprise you?

But he couldn't be more impressed with her, or admire her more than he already did. *But did she know that?* He did like the idea of a surprise, though. And he knew for a fact that she hated doing things she wasn't good at…maybe she was embarrassed, trying to save face.

He finally smiled. That was a habit he would coax her away from.

Still, if she wound up loving skydiving, it'd be the best thing for them. The rush, the thrill…the only thing that made him feel alive. Or at least, it was before he'd gotten to know her.

If she didn't understand his need for adrenaline, if she, like his parents, tried to pressure him out of it, or like the Club, suggested that he had a death wish, he didn't know how long their relationship would last.

That idea unnerved him.

She'll enjoy it, he told himself. And then the two of them would have adventures all over the world, with the Player's Club and without it. But even if she didn't, she'd accept him and what he needed.

I hope.

His phone rang, and he turned on the headset. "I'm driving."

"Finn, it's George."

"I'm driving," Finn repeated, and started to disconnect the call.

"Don't hang up!" The desperate tone in George's voice had Finn complying. "Listen, this is an emergency. Are you planning on skydiving today?"

"I'm headed for the airfield right now," Finn said. "But just to watch. I don't think I'm jumping today."

"Oh, thank God."

"What's up?" Finn would've given him a harder time, but there was something different, frantic, in George's voice. "You sound well and truly freaked out."

"Just don't go skydiving, okay?"

"Okay, now you're freaking *me* out. What's going on?"

George took a loud, shaky breath, and Finn heard the glug of a drink. "Your life's in danger, Finn."

Finn burst out laughing. "Well, you know me—"

"No. I mean somebody's trying to kill you."

Finn blinked. "Excuse me?"

"Damn it, I'm not joking!" George shrieked. He was usually a bellower, but fear ratcheted his voice up an octave. "This guy…Jonesy. He… I met him, and he came up with this plan for me to make some extra money, and damn it, the family owed me…. I was tired of being odd man out."

Finn rolled his eyes. "If this is your usual rant—"

"He came up with the plan." George rolled over his interruption. "The embezzlement plan."

Finn went cold. "You? You embezzled the money and framed Diana?" His hands gripped the steering wheel, but he wanted to strangle George's neck. "You idiot. We'd traced the fact that the funds had been embezzled, and we'd found that Victor guy. But we didn't know you were behind it all."

"Yeah, whatever," George said. "Fine. You can turn me in to Uncle Thorn, or the police, or whoever, I don't care. But the thing is, now he's tying up the loose ends."

"He who? What loose ends?"

"Jonesy," George spat. "The guy with the plan. The

guy who conned me." Now he sounded as if he was about to cry. "He knows you guys hacked into the network. He knows you're figuring it out. And I think...I think he's going to try to kill you. You and Diana both."

Finn's blood froze, his heart stopping. "Diana? What's he going to do to Diana?"

"I don't know. I don't know what his plans are for her," George said. "All I know is, he said something about skydiving today...an accident. I don't know how he'll get to her, but...but I don't want you guys to get killed." He was definitely crying. "I didn't want anybody to get killed. I just...I just wanted what was mine."

Skydiving.

Diana.

Finn floored the accelerator. The car screamed forward, tearing up the pavement.

"If anything happens to her, I'll kill you myself." Finn clicked off the phone, then frantically tried dialing Diana's phone, Lincoln's phone. Anyone.

No one answered.

DIANA TRIED TO wipe her palms, then wondered if the sweat would leave stains on the bright blue nylon jumpsuit she was wearing.

The sound of the plane was deafening—it wasn't that big, but the noise was simply insane, between the engines and the wind and everything. Finn told her that they used to do large group jumps, suggested that if she wanted, she might find it fun. She sincerely doubted it.

Lincoln leaned close to her ear. "We're about ready,"

he said, gesturing to her to stand in front of him. It was disturbingly intimate. He made sure that they were hooked together, since he'd be doing most of the actual "jump" part.

She'd merely be doing the plummeting-to-the-ground part.

Finn said this would be life-changing.

She wanted to see what Finn saw. She knew that he had his own reasons, that he was living each day as if it were his last because he didn't know if or when the cancer would decide to come back. She liked that he didn't seem to worry, only lived one day at a time. She didn't want to worry about how she was going to get another job, or dwell on the pain and stress of what Macalister's betrayal had done to her. She glanced at the open door of the plane and swallowed hard.

Well, she sure as hell wasn't worrying about all of that *now,* was she?

"I don't think I can do this," she murmured, but over the screaming wind, nobody heard her.

Lincoln had her all rigged up, and he held tight. It would've seemed almost romantic except that he was basically bellowing in her ear.

"All right, we'll move to the door now, okay?"

She didn't trust herself to speak without doing something embarrassing, like throwing up. So instead, she nodded. Then still had to be strongly nudged to get to the gaping door, with the air rushing by as if it were coming from a humungous industrial fan. Even the elements were telling her to stay in the damned plane.

You can do this. Just jump, quick, and get it over with. Hold your breath, close your eyes, and jump.

Oh, God. She swallowed hard, clutching at Lincoln behind her. Diana stared at all that ground…and all that empty space between it and her.

"Ready?" asked Lincoln.

She bit her lip. Held on tight. And then…

17

FINN'S CAR SCREECHED into the parking lot of the landing field. He had one hand on the steering wheel, the other on the redial button of his cell phone. He'd tried calling Diana, tried calling Lincoln. Had called the air control tower. "Tell them that there's a problem with the parachute! Tell them to cancel!"

They'd hung up on him, thinking he was a crackpot, which he no doubt sounded like. Finn was terrified.

He saw a plane high up in the distance. He thought he could make out the bright flash of a nylon jumpsuit. Were there two of them? A tandem jump?

He shut off the Porsche mindlessly and clambered out. *"No!"*

Like they could hear him. Like it would make a difference. He was running blindly. He saw them, circling, doing lazy loops. Almost a ballet. And any minute, they were going to try…

The chute opened, and they started spinning crazily, out of control. He held his breath. His lungs burned painfully. He couldn't look away.

They were twirling sideways, fast enough to cause nausea, disorientation. Then one of them put his hand up, and the chute was cut, flying away…and they were falling again. Falling like stones.

No, no, he thought. *I'm going to watch her die. Watch them die. Right now, right in front of me.*

His stomach seized up, and he fell to his knees. Another parachute opened. This time, the chute blossomed like a rose, blooming to its full capacity. They started dropping slowly now, still a little too quick, but they would be safe.

He released a long breath, then gulped in air, but still felt sick. He stood up, started running. It took countless minutes to get to where they'd finally tumbled, hitting the ground hard. He ran up to them.

"Thank God, I thought I'd lost you," he said, pulling the chute off and lunging to embrace them.

"We thought you'd lost us, too, mate." A thick Australian accent surprised him. "But unless you're going to buy me dinner, I'd say stop hugging so tight."

Finn stepped back, dazed. Unless Diana had grown a handlebar mustache and Lincoln was black, he had the wrong people.

"Sorry," he said, staggering away. "I…I thought…"

The guy with the mustache nodded, getting to his feet. "You're thinking we were somebody you loved. I get it." He shook his head. "Nope, just us. But there's a plane landing over there…maybe she's on that?"

Finn waved his thanks, and dashed toward the other aircraft. If there had been an accident, a skydiving fatality, there would be emergency vehicles here, his mind reasoned, even as his legs pumped faster. Or was the parachute thing a mistake? He wouldn't care if George was messing with him. Wouldn't care if it was an elaborate hoax. All he cared about was Diana being all right.

The plane taxied to a stop, and Finn froze again, his mind racing, his body paralyzed with fear. The door opened, and Diana stepped out, her blue nylon jumpsuit still on. Lincoln exited behind her. She looked tearful, but her chin went up.

"I didn't jump," she said immediately, as she walked up to him. Her tone was defensive. "I couldn't. I was terrified. And I know how much the Club means to you, and I know how much you wanted us to be this thrill-seeking couple. But I just..."

She shut up when he crushed her against him, needing to feel her in his arms. Needing to physically know she was okay. "Finn. I can't breathe."

He eased off a bit, and knew his eyes were watering a little.

"Finn," she said, as she noticed, stroking his cheeks. "Are you all right?"

He glanced over at Lincoln, who was also staring at him with concern. "It was George," Finn said. "George and someone else set Diana up. Somebody else with more brains and less scruples."

"Easy to find the former," Lincoln mused, "not so easy the latter. So?"

"So George's associate managed to have your parachute sabotaged."

Lincoln's eyebrows went up, and Diana paled. Finn

held her tighter. "I thought I was going to lose you," he said, and his voice broke. "I have never been so scared in my life."

"Nothing happened," she said, kissing him, hugging him back fiercely. "I'm fine. I'm not going anywhere." She held his face in her hands, her eyes bright. "I'm not leaving you."

He held her for a long minute. Then he needed to show her, and himself, just how alive they both were. He took her hand, all but dragging her to the car. Lincoln simply laughed. Finn didn't care.

"FINN, I'M ALL RIGHT," Diana reassured him, but her heart was pounding. She'd felt so close to death herself at the open hatch door, with the world so far below her.... She suddenly, overwhelmingly, wanted to be with Finn.

Next thing she knew, they were sprinting toward his car, pausing only to take her jumpsuit off and leave it at the hangar. She shivered in anticipation.

"I don't think we'll last the hour drive it'll take to get to one of our houses," Finn rasped, his eyes dark with desire. "I feel badly, but...maybe a motel?"

"Anywhere," she said breathlessly. "Just *hurry*."

She stroked the inside of his thigh, tracing the inseam up to his crotch.

Finn let out a strangled sound. "*Now* you get the adrenaline rush."

She laughed. He moved his hand to place her palm on the hard length of his cock beneath the denim of his jeans. She purred.

"Damn it," he breathed. "We're not even going to make it to a motel."

They drove about ten minutes, then he pulled off onto a dirt road, the car bumping along the uneven surface. They stopped behind a barn, and a series of empty corrals well out of sight of the road. Finn shut off the engine.

"This place only opens for the rodeo, and this is the wrong season," he said, reaching for her. "I don't think they'll mind."

She giggled, unbuckling her seat belt. "Ride 'em, cowboy," she invited, undoing her jeans.

He groaned…then immediately made a sound of pain as he got caught on the stick shift. They both burst into laughter.

"Backseat," he muttered, getting out. She clambered over the reclined seat, shimmying out of her pants on the way. Given how she was feeling, the whole world could have been watching from the rodeo bleachers, and she wouldn't have cared. She felt reckless, wild, excited.

Finn shucked off his jeans, eyes gleaming as he got into the backseat.

"Touch me," she said, opening herself to him. And he covered her, fitting himself between her spread legs. He entered her in one slow glide, filling her completely, and she moaned in gratitude, wrapping her legs around him.

He withdrew, then drove her deeper into the leather seat. She gripped him tighter, clawing at his naked back. She could feel the seams of the seat pressing into her skin. They bumped against the interior, her head hanging slightly out of the open door. She didn't care. It felt primal.

Finn licked and kissed her collarbone, and increased his tempo. She raised her hips to meet every thrust. He was bucking now, their bodies moving like mating animals. Her breathing was punctuated by sharp sighs of pleasure as he massaged her breasts and rolled his hips in the way that made her mindless with need.

Unable to hold it in any longer, she called out to him, the orgasm sending her over the edge. Immediately, he paused—his whole body tense—to let her ride it out. When she had, she got onto her knees, and he entered her. The friction felt different. Though the same desire coursed through her. He pulled her hips flush against his pelvis and buried himself in her, she backed against him, wanting him. His chest covered her, and he slid over her, time and again, as he pushed and withdrew, rubbing her breasts and stroking her hips while she arched her back.

His breathing was growing uneven now—he was close. She moved hard against him, rubbing her own clit and moaning his name. She felt the second orgasm beginning to roll through her like thunder. He thrust hard inside her, his hips moving like a piston as he came.

In the aftermath, they collapsed in a heap.

"How're you feeling?" he asked, gasping.

"That'll tide me over till we get home." She laughed like a kid, too loud and a tiny bit hysterical. So this, she thought, was what it felt like to be invincible. She sent him a loopy, glorious smile.

"I love you," he said, stroking her face.

She was surprised that tears pricked her eyes. "Finn, you..."

"I didn't understand, not until..." He shook, as if he couldn't bear to say it. "I love you. I wouldn't have gone through all this with you if I didn't, and I don't ever want to think about losing you."

"Even if I don't do the things you do?" she said, feeling foolish.

He nodded. "I love you for who you are. Not for what you do."

She felt a warm sense of happiness expanding in her chest. "I love you, too, Finn." She kissed him, softly, with deepening intensity, until he pulled back.

"I'll be more careful," he said. "But...I still need to..."

She stopped him with another kiss. "I love you for who you are," she repeated. "Not for what you do."

A DAY LATER, FINN brought Diana with him to see his parents. They'd invited him to the big house in Marin, rather than the cold, confrontational environment of Macalister Enterprises.

He wanted Diana to accompany him, because he felt they owed her an apology. Not that he was expecting one.

He could feel Diana's discomfort as they walked through the grand foyer of the mansion and the butler took their coats. "It's all right, Di," he whispered, hugging her. "We'll tell them what we know. We'll get this all sorted out."

She seemed ready to burst. "Are you going to tell them I'm your girlfriend?" she blurted.

Of all the things... He grinned, feeling relief sweep away the tension. "Hell, yes," he said, kissing her neck and holding her despite her squirming attempts to get away. "In fact, I'm going to call you Honeybuns. I think you should call me Schmoopy-pants."

She laughed, which he'd hoped. "That's Ms. Honeybuns to you, pal," she said, even though her eyes were shining. And she let him take her hand and lead her to the stately living room.

His mother was wearing one of her more casual outfits; his father was wearing a Macalister Enterprises polo and a pair of khakis. So it was supposed to be low-key. Too bad you could cut the new tension in the air with a chain saw.

"Son," his mother said, her voice tremulous.

He sat down on the couch next to her, giving her a hug. "Mom," he said. "It's okay."

She looked like she was ready to weep; instead, she smiled and cast a glance at Diana. "And Ms. Song. I'm so sorry for all of this trouble. George has been here, and he explained everything."

Finn growled. "Oh, has he?"

"Yes, he has." His father, clearly pensive, sounded somber. "Just before the police took him away."

Diana's eyes seemed to practically pop out of her head. Finn quickly got up and stood by her, holding her hand. She gripped his hand tightly. "He was arrested?" she asked softly.

"Yes. He turned in the others—Victor, and a shady

man named Jonesy. At least, that was the name he was using." His father stared intensely at Diana. "If I get my hands on that man..."

"The police have," Finn reminded him. "So that's what's important."

"He was going to kill you," his mother breathed. The tears welled up. "Kill you both."

"Yes, we know," Diana said, and in comparison, her voice was cool, calm. "But he didn't, Mrs. Macalister. So am I to understand that my name is cleared?"

His father all but choked. "I guess I owe you an apology, Diana."

"You think?" Finn sniped, but Diana stilled him by squeezing his hand hard.

Thorn made a face at him, but then kept his attention on Diana. "I don't apologize very often. You know that, Diana." He crossed his arms, in that moment looking more like a bouncer than the CEO of a multibillion-dollar company. "So let's let bygones be bygones. It was a mistake, an easy one to make. You can't honestly blame me."

"Actually, I can." Diana's voice was still mild as milk. But her expression was hard as steel. Finn was impressed.

My girl's got guts, he thought, as his father frowned.

"Listen, I made a mistake," Thorn repeated. "But I'm not going to beg you to come back. If you want to be pissy about me protecting my company, then I guess your loyalty's not what I thought it was. Maybe you shouldn't come back."

There it was. The hot button—the most sensitive chink in Diana's armor. Finn couldn't stay quiet at that.

"Diana is one of the most loyal people I know," Finn said defiantly. "And I don't see any reason why she should be loyal to someone who would throw her under the bus at the first sign of trouble, without even trying to let her defend herself."

"It's all right, Finn," she said, and to his surprise, she really did seem all right. "It's easier this way, anyway."

Thorn's scowl was like a thunderstorm. "I'm not playing a game here, Diana."

"Neither am I." She smiled congenially and extended her hand to shake Thorn's. He was shocked enough to take it. "I can't thank you enough for all the experience you've given me, and for paying for my education. I'm sorry that we couldn't go further, but in fact, right now is probably the perfect time for you to bring up some new blood and make some changes. I'll always think of you fondly."

Thorn's mouth fell open. Finn felt like applauding… but didn't.

"So that's it, then," Thorn said, as Diana started to turn to walk away. Then he addressed Finn. "What about you? Do you have some flowery 'screw you' speech for us, as well? Going to go live the life of a happy pauper and cliff dive or something?"

Finn went over to his father and hugged him. Thorn could not have been more shocked if he'd punched him in the gut.

"I'm sorry, Dad," he said. "I mean that. I recently… I finally felt what it is you feel like when I do the stuff I do. I never really understood it. Not until Diana almost died."

His father went rigid. Then he crushed Finn in a bear hug.

"If anything happened to you..." his dad said, his voice rough with pure emotion. "Finn, I don't want to be stupid about this, but if you'd just do things my way."

"Even if I did things your way, I wouldn't necessarily be safe," Finn said, prying himself from his father's protective arms. He hugged his mother gently. "I'll be more aware of what I'm doing, but I'm not going to live in some prison so you'll feel better. But I will be more careful, and I will let you know what I'm doing."

Thorn looked like he was about to bellow. "Damn it, Finn—"

"Thorn! That's enough."

Finn and Thorn both stared at the woman seated on the French Provincial sofa, drying her eyes. Finn's mother sat ramrod straight, looking every bit a queen.

"How long have you been trying to run Finn's life, Thorn? And how's that been working out for you?" Her voice was firm. "I don't want Finn to risk his life foolishly, but I'm not stupid enough to cut him out simply because he won't do what we want. He's making a fair compromise here, Thorn. Stop being such a hard-ass."

Thorn goggled.

"Mom?" Finn was torn between laughing and gaping openmouthed.

"I don't stand up to him all that often, but this is important." She got up, kissed Thorn on the cheek...and leveled a steely gaze at him. "I'm tired of being upset.

I'm tired of *all* of this. And if you really want to press this, then you and I are going to have an issue, Thorn." She let that statement sink in. "You don't want that to happen, do you?"

"Uh, no," Thorn said, obviously appalled.

Diana giggled. Finn started laughing.

"So, would you two kids like to join us for dinner?" his mother asked, as if the previous five minutes had never happened.

"Um..." Finn looked at Diana. "What do you think?"

"Some other time," Diana said graciously, looping her arm with Finn's. "We've got to go."

"Really?" Finn said, as they headed from the room. "Where to?"

"On a vacation," she said. "I don't know about you, but I really, really need one."

18

Two weeks later

DIANA STRETCHED OUT on a lounge chair. The sun beat down, warming her skin. She could smell guava and tropical flowers surrounding her, and hear the soft lapping sound of the waves on the private beach below. The breeze caressed her skin.

"Okay, let's go over this again," Finn said in the background, and she saw his shadow as he paced across the deck with his cell phone in hand. "We'll need to figure out how big we want this to be, and private membership, and nonprofit status…did somebody get the nonprofit thing?"

"Finn…" she said with warning, closing her eyes behind her sunglasses. "You promised you'd only be on for five minutes."

"Just a sec…" he said to her, and she laughed. "All right, we're going to have to wrap this up, guys, but I do want to make sure that if we're starting a Player's Club that's open to the public, that it absolutely kicks ass and…yes, I know, I've got that file here somewhere."

Diana sat up, sighing. She never should've suggested that he take the Player's Club public. Still, he was more motivated than she'd ever seen him. He and Lincoln were like two kids. Two kids that fought a lot, admittedly, but they were also terribly excited.

Good grief. If she wasn't careful, he'd turn into a workaholic.

She snickered at the thought. Then she waited to catch his eye. He held up a finger in the universal "just one minute" gesture. "So finally, let's look over the revenue projections…"

She sighed again. Then, smiling, she reached behind her back and untied the bikini top, letting the triangles of fabric fall to the deck.

Finn eyed her move, and he smiled. "Um, guys? Gotta go. Bye."

He tossed the phone onto a table and strode over to her with purpose, leaning down and stretching out next to her on the large lounge chair. "Well, *this* is more like it."

"I thought you were going to work the whole time," she said, with mock complaint, as she giggled when he took one nipple into his mouth.

"Nonsense. Just wanted to take care of a few details." He smiled against her skin. "You know I'm a details kind of guy."

"Oh?" She shuddered when his fingers slipped inside

her bikini bottoms. "I've got some details for you to look over...."

"My favorite kind," he said, and kissed her.

* * * * *

PASSION

COMING NEXT MONTH

AVAILABLE APRIL 10, 2012

#2149 FEELING THE HEAT

The Westmorelands

Brenda Jackson

Dr. Micah Westmoreland knows Kalina Daniels hasn't forgiven him. But he can't ignore the heat that still burns between them....

#2150 ON THE VERGE OF I DO

Dynasties: The Kincaids

Heidi Betts

#2151 HONORABLE INTENTIONS

Billionaires and Babies

Catherine Mann

#2152 WHAT LIES BENEATH

Andrea Laurence

#2153 UNFINISHED BUSINESS

Cat Schield

#2154 A BREATHLESS BRIDE

The Pearl House

Fiona Brand

You can find more information on upcoming Harlequin® titles, free excerpts and more at www.Harlequin.com.

HDCNM0312

Taft Bowman knew he'd ruined any chance he'd had for happiness with Laura Pendleton when he drove her away years ago...and into the arms of another man, thousands of miles away. Now she was back, a widow with two small children...and despite himself, he was starting to believe in second chances.

Harlequin Special® Edition® presents a new installment in USA TODAY *bestselling author RaeAnne Thayne's miniseries,* THE COWBOYS OF COLD CREEK.

Enjoy a sneak peek of A COLD CREEK REUNION

Available April 2012 from Harlequin® Special Edition®

A younger woman stood there, and from this distance he had only a strange impression, as though she was somehow standing on an island of calm amid the chaos of the scene, the flashing lights of the emergency vehicles, shouts between his crew members, the excited buzz of the crowd.

And then the woman turned and he just about tripped over a snaking fire hose somebody shouldn't have left there.

Laura.

He froze, and for the first time in fifteen years as a firefighter, he forgot about the incident, his mission, just what the hell he was doing here.

Laura.

Ten years. He hadn't seen her in all that time, since the week before their wedding when she had given him back his ring and left town. Not just town. She had left the whole damn country, as if she couldn't run far enough to

HSEEXP0412

get away from him.

Some part of him desperately wanted to think he had made some kind of mistake. It couldn't be her. That was just some other slender woman with a long sweep of honey-blond hair and big, blue, unforgettable eyes. But no. It was definitely Laura. Sweet and lovely.

Not his.

He was going to have to go over there and talk to her. He didn't want to. He wanted to stand there and pretend he hadn't seen her. But he was the fire chief. He couldn't hide out just because he had a painful history with the daughter of the property owner.

Sometimes he hated his job.

Will Taft and Laura be able to make the years recede...or is the gulf between them too broad to ever cross?

Find out in
A COLD CREEK REUNION
Available April 2012 from Harlequin® Special Edition®
wherever books are sold.

HSEEXP0412